Other Titles by Kristopher Rufty

BONE CHIMES

KRISTOPHER RUFTY

Bone Chimes
This edition © 2024
Copyright © 2017/2024 by Kristopher Rufty
Cover Design © 2024

The Chomper, appeared in *Splatterpunk Magazine #7, © 2015. Love Seat* appeared with *Last One Alive,* © 2013.
Bedside Manner, appeared in *Extreme Horror* from Festa-Verlag, © 2016.
Gearhart's Wife appeared with *Last One Alive* and in *Sets Quartet,* © 2016 from Thunderstorm Books.
The Night Everything Changed © 2011, originally from Samhain Publishing.

ISBN: 9781546886761

DEDICATION

For Mrs. Moody and Ms. Brown.
Thank you for your support.

TABLE OF CONTENTS

ACKNOWLEDGEMENTS

*T*here are a lot of folks to thank. Plenty of people have read my stories through the years, each offering their own bits of encouragement and opinions. But I'm going to narrow it down some for this collection and hope the rest will forgive me this time.

I would like to start with my eighth-grade English teacher, Mrs. Moody. Other than my parents, you were the first person to tell me I could do great things with my writing. I still have the yearbook with your special note of encouragement inside. I will never forget it.

Special thanks to Ms. Brown for showing me the bookcases you kept out of sight. And thank you for allowing me to borrow titles to help influence my own writing. I hate you never got to read any of my published work. You are incredibly missed.

Countless thanks must go to my parents for allowing me to write such wild stories to begin with. Thank you, Mom, for taking them with you to work to read on your lunchbreaks. Thank you, Dad, for bringing home that old typewriter when you saw how desperately I needed to write. Another thank you for the word processor many years later. And I must also thank you for introducing me to the word "rump." It was because of you that I started using it in my own writing.

Next, I want to thank Evans Light, David Bernstein, Tod Clark, Tim Waggoner, Jeff Strand, Hunter Shea, Jonathan Janz, Don D'Auria, Tristan Thorne, Brian Keene, Bryan Smith, Trent Haaga,

Wrath James White, Kim Myers, Erin Sweet-Al Mehairi, Paul Goblirsch, Paul Synuria II, Gary MacDonald, Deborah Grace, Aleka Nakis, Kathleen Pickering, Evan Pickering, Traci Hall, and Heather Graham. Every one of you has been a crucial part of it all. And a very special thanks to Ronald Malfi for helping me with titling this collection. I'm proud to call you all my friends.

INTRODUCTION

I remember when I first picked up a copy of *Angel Board*. The author was someone I hadn't heard of, but his book was part of a new horror line. A few pages in and, despite Dorchester being extinct, I could've sworn I was reading another classic horror title. I thought maybe it was a reprint of something I had missed out on. I was wrong. It was new, and from a new talent. I gobbled that novel up and realized I'd found a new favorite author. I was blown away at how much I enjoyed *Angel Board*. From that point on, I made sure to read everything Kristopher Rufty released.

I met Krist sometime in 2011, if I remember correctly. It had been online. He'd been published with Samhain, and I had a novel in the pipeline with them. Krist and I hit it off immediately. He was uber helpful and supportive. We wound up chatting about writing and how we couldn't believe we were published with authors we'd been reading for years, as well as how great it was to be working with Don D'Auria. But we also chatted about regular life and that's where the friendship solidified. Krist is one of the nicest, most sincere and genuine people I've met. I'm honored to call him my friend.

We kept in touch regularly and wound up co-writing a novella with Shane McKenzie and Adam Cesare. What a blast that was! We met in real life shortly after that at Scares that Care 2, and continue to talk and meet up at the convention every year.

Well, enough about that. Let's talk about Krist's work.

3

The man can write, and write with the best of them. I know it's said about many writers, but when I say Krist pulls no punches and writes from his gut, he truly does. Sure, he gives us horror fiends plenty of delicious bloodshed and gore, but more than that, he stirs up emotions. He knows how to scare, knows how to wrench your heart out and make you feel sympathy for his characters. He touches upon real life with his fiction. But he doesn't stop there. No. You think you know where one of his stories is going... You think you know who is safe... Just when you think the road is going to turn left, it whips right and slopes down at a 90-degree angle and drops you into a pit of blood-caked and bone-ridden spikes. There is *no* relaxing when reading a Rufty tale. This is made clear in any of his titles, but the one that haunts me the most is *A Dark Autumn*—a novella that took me on a roller coaster and then turned that coaster upside down. My emotions were all over the place—and that's what I want from the authors I read. His horror has heart and stays with the reader long after the pages are done being turned. He was born a writer and storyteller. If you've read him before, you already know this. And if this is your first go-round to Krist's world, then I welcome you with chainsaws a' wielding and knives a' slicing.

With *Bone Chimes*, Krist hits all the right buttons and shows off his chops yet again. This collection is a dark journey (with some laughs) through Krist's incredibly imaginary mind and is an excellent potpourri of his work. He's written novellas, novels, and directed films, so it was only natural we got a short story collection from him. Took him long enough, didn't it? Well, it was worth the wait!

Well, I've taken up enough of your reading time, so turn the page and enjoy *Bone Chimes*, a wonderfully, dark and creepy collection of horror tales.

David Bernstein, 2017

AUTHOR'S NOTE

As I was writing the first draft of *Angel Board* way back in 2009, I read Bentley Little's *The Collection* for the first time. I'd read a lot of short story collections and anthologies before it, and plenty since, but I still believe that Little's collection is the best of all. I learned so much from each story inside, and it also restored my love of writing short fiction. Since then, I've tried to write a couple short stories between each novel I complete. Something to keep me writing, but nothing too heavy that would require a ton of my time. Sometimes, I didn't get the chance because as soon as I turned in a novel, I had to jump right into another one because of previously made commitments.

Whenever I did get to work on some stories, whether they were good or bad, I kept them. Even if they weren't finished, I held onto everything. I never throw out anything. No matter how much hell the story put me through, or how frustrated it made me.

This short story collection was pitched to my old editor. He liked the idea, so I got to work, gathering up stories to send him that I thought he might like. But before we could get very far on it, he was released from the original publisher. Feeling discouraged, I tucked it away for over a year, with a lot of doubt I'd ever return to it. It kept nagging me, though, until I finally couldn't ignore it any longer. Besides, I'd already talked about the collection in a few interviews. Eventually, people would start asking what happened to it.

What the heck? I thought. Might as well finish putting it together.

Decided to get back to work on it, I thought it might be a neat idea to include one story I wrote from each year after I read Little's *The Collection* for the first time. Like I said earlier, I tried to write a couple stories between each novel, so there was a decent supply to sift through. To my surprise, not all of them were extremely terrible. I wanted to include so many that I actually had to cut a few to keep the count low. I didn't want to throw together a large boxset of stories all at once. Keeping it simple and small was what I decided on and I hope it was the right choice.

I should point out, though, that some of the previously released stories did come out in some form of publication during the same years, but they were written separately, and I felt they still fit the concept I was trying to follow.

I hope you enjoy these little shattered glimpses of my imagination. It can be a fun place to play, though the woods that border the playground just might be filled with monsters.

THE CHOMPER

A pleasant melody of chimes played through the house. But to me, the song was like fingernails on a chalkboard. It was just after noon, and I was sitting at my desk, polishing chapter fourteen of my new book.

No doubt, Ms. Needlemire was at the door.

The soft taps of footsteps resounded from the hallway. Monica appeared in the doorway, worry wrinkling her forehead. Her sunshine-colored hair was pulled back, hanging in a loose ponytail. Strands draggled in her face. She had on a gray tank top and athletic shorts that left her tawny legs looking very bare. In one hand, she held a squirt bottle of cleaning fluid. In the other hand was a soiled rag.

"Don't worry," I said.

My words did nothing to relax her strained face. She looked distressed. "Tomorrow's Sunday."

"I know. There's a calendar on my desk."

"Don't get snarky, Adam," she said, stepping back so I could get by.

My tone was deliberate. Monica had been on me for two weeks about Ms. Needlemire. Each day seemed a bit worse. Today my wife had been a wreck.

Pausing partway up the hall, I turned back, feeling guilty. Monica watched me like a child not wanting her father to leave for work. It looked as if the doorway to my office had swallowed half of her, only showing the right side of her body.

"I'm sorry," I said.

"Are you really going to answer the door?" Monica asked, ignoring my apology.

"I figured I would."

Monica nibbled her lip. A quiet whine escaped her mouth.

"We can't avoid her," I said. "She lives down the street, for Christ's sake."

"She's here to talk about the envelope."

"I'll handle it," I said, turning away from Monica. I glimpsed her squeezing the squirt bottle hard enough to spray the doorway paneling.

Ms. Needlemire had come over every third Saturday of the three months we'd lived in Golden Gates Community. Each visit had been the same: a reminder that the envelope would arrive and tell us our tithe. This time would be different. She probably knew the cream-colored envelope had been left on our doorstep two weeks ago.

I opened the door, squinting at the bright sunlight. As my eyes adjusted, I began to make out the minute shape of a flowery blue dress. A pallid wrinkled face, frowning underneath crusty red lipstick, came into focus. The eyes, tiny dull marbles, looked overly large behind the thick black glasses. Her ash-colored hair puffed out on both sides of her head underneath the flowery hat.

The clumpy red lips spread into a smile. "Hello, Mr. Schaffer."

"Ms. Needlemire. How are you this morning?"

"It's past noon, Mr. Schaffer. Hardly could be considered morning."

"Right," I said. "My fault. Good afternoon."

"It's a hot one today, isn't it?" she said. "Or have you been keeping yourself too busy writing another one of those violent crime novels to enjoy the day God gave us?"

Like a champ, I smiled. I was used to people criticizing my stories. "My work is my joy, Ms. Needliemire, so I haven't missed a thing."

Ms. Needlemire stared at me, eyes locked on mine. The sun glinted off the thick glass lenses like water. I could tell she was waiting on me to get it started. When she finally figured out I wasn't going to, she sighed. "Have you begun the preparations for what we discussed?"

"I'm working on it."

"Tomorrow's the third Sunday, Mr. Schaffer. This will be your first blood offering. If you wish to placate the Chomper, then you have to make sure everything's in order."

"It will be."

"I don't believe you. And may I remind you that you signed the contract. The hazards of not obeying the Chomper's creeds…"

"That's not necessary," I said, stopping her.

Ignoring me, she said, "The Chomper allowed us to build our homes on this land. In return, we tithe every third Sunday of every month. This is something we give in obedience to the Chomper for what it's allowed. Since you're new here, you were given a reprieve. Now it's time for you to begin your tithe."

My tithe. Jesus.

"Do you hear yourself?" I asked.

"I hear myself just fine. Unlike my eyes, my ears are in pristine shape. You knew what this community had committed to before you bought the house, before you signed the contract."

"Guess I slept through the blood offering meeting."

Ms. Needlemire lowered her head, letting out a long breath that rattled her craggy cheeks. When she looked up, her eyes somehow looked darker. "Mr. Schaffer, I'm going to be frank with you. Many neighbors did not want you to come here. This is a community of families that love each other. You and your wife have no family, and from talking with Mrs. Schaffer, have no plans of starting one anytime soon."

That had been Monica's decision, not mine. I'd wanted kids for a couple years now. Each time I brought it up, there was a different reason why we couldn't. Our apartment was too small. We didn't make enough money. When two of my books were turned into successful movies, my advances got bigger, as did my royalty checks, resolving the money issue. Then I moved us into this house tucked away in a small community surrounded by woods. An area without crime, the perfect place to raise children. Now Monica wanted us to get settled in for a while, get used to the house, our neighbors.

Maybe next year.

I didn't share any of this with Ms. Needlemire. It wasn't her business to know it.

Frowning, Ms. Needlemire continued, "And your novels are so…grim. Every page chocked full of fornication and violence."

"They're crime stories. That's sort of the norm. And thank you for reading them."

"That's not normal to most of us here at Golden Gates. But it was put to a vote, and by one vote, you were accepted. Bring in some youth, they'd said. It'd be good for the neighborhood, getting people to continue the tithe long after we're gone. Stupid. Youth doesn't believe in anything unless it can be explained from top to bottom in every way. There's no faith, no credence."

"So we're here to replace the ones about to die?"

"Precisely."

"Don't you think this shit is…crazy?"

Ms. Needlemire frowned. "We knew what had to be done before my husband built our house with his bare hands. We'd made a pact with the Chomper, all of us in the community. There's no other place any of us would rather live, no other place worth living. So you take the good with the bad, and learn to live with it. My husband, God rest his soul, would agree."

"I pay a mortgage, which should be enough."

"I know you received your envelope. What was inside is your tithe, every third Sunday."

"The hell it is. Do you have any idea what was *in* the envelope?"

Ms. Needlemire threw up her hand. The skin of her fingers looked as if she'd been washing dishes for a long time. "That's not for me to know. It's *your* tithe. If you tell it to me, then the Chomper will be angry with us both. No matter what, never tell anyone what it is."

"And if I don't give it the tithe it wants…"

"You breach your contact and can move, or offer something in its place in hopes for forgiveness."

"Like a chicken or something?"

"Something of yours, with blood."

I couldn't believe this creepy nonsense. What scared me the most was how much Ms. Needlemire believed it. Probably everybody else in the neighborhood did too. I had no desire to play along. Yes, we'd signed the contract. We'd been told about Chompers and tithes and blood, but it had meant nothing. Living here was what mattered. Monica said, no matter what, we had to have this house.

And the community offered lawn care.

Forget it. I'd cut my own damn grass.

"Thanks for stopping by, Ms. Needlemire. I need to get back to work."

As I started to shut the door, Ms. Needlemire stomped her foot against it. "I really hope you learn to take this seriously. I'd hate to see you go. I was the final vote that got you in here." Ms. Needlemire turned away from me, and shuffled down the three steps to the sidewalk.

Standing in the doorway, I watched her sluggishly walk away. Hunched over, her left arm was out, as if holding an imaginary person's hand.

Or a ghost's.

That thought sent a sharp chill up my spine. I shut the door.

In the kitchen, I opened the fridge and took out a bottle of beer. Twisting off the cap, there was a carbonated *pop* that speckled my hand with cold dots. I guzzled.

"A little early, isn't it?" Monica asked from behind me.

Gulping, I shook my head.

"Are you going to tithe now?" she asked.

Lowering the bottle, I quietly belched. "Are you insane? No."

Rolling her eyes, Monica leaned against the doorway. She no longer had the cleaning products. "It's expected of us."

"We're going to disappoint a lot of people."

"What if they make us move? And I can't go. I *can't*."

"We *own* this house."

"But the contract…"

"Screw the contract. They can't make us move. We own the house, the land. Right?"

Monica, closing her eyes, nodded. When she opened them, I noticed wetness making them shimmer. "Right." There was no conviction in her voice, only a quality that hinted at how concerned she was.

"What do *you* think we should do?" I asked.

"I…" Groaning, she looked at the fridge, marching forward. She plucked the envelope from behind the magnet on the door. The small magnetic disc hit the floor and bounced, sounding like a pebble. "We give it what it wants."

Though the paper was tucked inside the envelope, I could plainly see the crude, ink-drawn image of our tithe.

A child.

Sunday dragged on. Monica stayed in the bedroom all day. I tried working on the revisions for my newest novel, but had trouble concentrating. I made a sandwich for supper. My plate was still mostly full when I finished. We had no dog to eat the scraps.

A rule of Golden Gates—no pets. Too many had disappeared, breaking families' hearts. Now pets were no longer allowed.

Sitting on the back porch, I puffed on a cigar, watching the sun sink behind the trees. The lower it got, the more my stomach hurt. When darkness surpassed the day, I was sick with dread. Even my forehead felt stretched and tingly.

I stubbed out the cigar in the ash tray on the table beside me, stood, and went inside.

Monica was in bed when I went into the bedroom, but not asleep. She leaned against the pillows, her head on the headboard. She had on my favorite white gown. A sheer thing that barely reached her thighs; her tanned skin was dark smears behind it. I could see the contours of her breasts, the dots of her turgid nipples. Feet crossed at the ankles, her calf bulged out. The light made a small, glimmering puddle on her lotion-fresh skin. Her thick auburn hair hung around her shoulders.

Though I was kind of mad at her, I felt myself becoming aroused.

Ignoring her, I headed to the bathroom. Took a quick shower, brushed my teeth, and combed my hair. I grabbed my robe from the back of the door, and threw it on, tying the belt in the front.

When I left the bathroom, I entered a room suffused in candlelight. Shadows writhed on the walls. Looking at the bed, I saw Monica had shed the gown. Naked, she lay on her side, leg bent, knee on the mattress. Her hand rubbed circles on the sheet.

Staring up at me, her eyes looked hopeful and a little nervous. She didn't speak. Didn't need to. I untied the knot, pulled my arms out of the robe. It dropped at my feet. I climbed onto the bed, positioning myself above her. As I crawled closer, her legs spread, opening up for me. I put an elbow down on either side of her head, angled my hips, and rammed into her.

Monica sucked in a deep breath, tilting back her head. We didn't kiss, only stared at each other as I slammed over and over. Monica gasped under me as the headboard pounded the wall. My savage lunges brought her to a quick shuddering release. I felt myself begin to swell, preparing for the final burst.

Light blasted through the window. It shone as if a spotlight had been aimed at our house, killing the romantic candlelight. Squealing, Monica slapped at my shoulders. I tumbled off her. My back hit the mattress as Monica flung herself off the bed. She ran to the window, rump flexing. Though the curtains were closed, light shoved in, giving the wispy fabric a ghostly glow. Monica was a dark contour in front of the window.

"Get away from there," I said. My testicles ached. "Somebody'll see."

"What the hell is that?"

"Bright light." I sat up, swinging my legs over the mattress. I found my robe on the floor. Throwing it on, I stood up. "I'm going to see what the hell's going on."

Monica spun around, emitting a hysterical gasp. "You can't go out! It's after midnight!"

"The hell with the rules," I said.

That was another one from the Golden Gates policy. Nobody could venture outdoors after midnight, without prior approval. They said it was out of respect for your neighbors. That way you wouldn't wake them up by sneaking around.

Monica said, "Don't you hear it?"

Pausing halfway across the room, I listened. I heard the low grumble of a clanking engine. I heard hissing spurts of air, like an old train. I heard the deep whopping sound a helicopter about to take flight might make.

Joining Monica, I pulled back the curtain enough to peek out. I was momentarily blinded by the garish luster pointed right at us.

"Sounds like a semi," I said.

"What's it doing out there?"

Watching us, I thought. But I said nothing.

For ten minutes, Monica and I stared out the window, at the light that seemed to be raptly fixated on just us. Whatever was causing that light was angry at Monica and me.

I shivered.

The engine revved a few times. Smoke wafted across the light, curling in dark tendrils. Gears clinked and squeaked, the noise changing pitch as the light began to shrink. Soon, it was hardly there at all. The room darkened. Then the light was gone.

Only the carroty smolder of the candles remained.

I snuck out of bed as daylight was just beginning to thin the darkness. I had a limited window to do what I wanted. Quietly rushing downstairs, I entered my office. I quickly dressed in the clothes I'd hidden under my desk after Monica had finally fallen asleep.

Then I slipped out of the house.

The morning was cool and damp, only a hint of uncomfortable summer heat waiting to burst through. The mild temperature would burn off quickly when the sun broke through the clouds. But that was fine, since I planned on being back at home long before that happened.

At the end of our driveway, I turned left, hurrying up the road. Woods bordered either side, shading the blacktop enough to make it look bottomless. I wondered if I should've brought a flashlight.

As I walked, I noticed there were no sounds from the woods. No birds. No scuttles. Only a hollow silence that made my ears buzz.

The Duggins' house was the first on the right, beyond the woods. It was a lovely, two-story home with a wraparound porch. Plants hung from the porch's ceiling all over like slings of garlic. A stone path led from the porch, cutting a curvy line through the grass. The driveway had been designed of identical stone.

The dew-drenched grass glistened around a dark spot in the front yard. From where I stood in the road, this small patch looked scorched, but it was hard to tell for sure. I needed a closer look.

I gave a quick glance in both directions, saw nobody was out, and trotted into the front yard. The dew soaked through my shoes, making my socks feel sloshy. With each step, I looked around. Nobody watched from the house. The windows were dark. Reaching the begrimed patch of grass, my anus tightened into a ball.

The grass was soaked in fresh blood. Ribbons of what looked like flesh stretched like webbing. I checked other houses, finding similar stains. Sometimes I found clumpy brown bits sprinkled on top of slushy piles like gross ice cream.

By the time I reached Ms. Needlemire's house where the road dead-ended, the morning was filled with light. I needed to head back home, but I couldn't without checking her yard.

Even as I approached the front, I saw the familiar smear in the grass. I didn't bother checking for anybody as I trespassed onto her property.

"My God," I muttered.

Bone fragments covered the grass like gray mulch.

"You've seen it," said Ms. Needlemire.

Jumping back, I nearly shouted in surprise. I looked at the porch. Ms. Needlemire sat in a rocking chair, a cup of coffee resting on her knee. Steam curled up to her face. She was blanketed in shadow, but her glasses shone like twin flashlights.

"What's going on, Ms. Needlemire? What is all this?"

"You didn't tithe, did you?"

I didn't answer. The tone of her voice suggested she already knew.

"You got off with a warning this time," she said. "A month from now, you better have the tithe it wants, or you won't make it to regret it."

"What does that mean?"

"You're smart, Mr. Schaffer. You know what I mean."

I did know.

"Just do what the Chomper wants. You'll be fine."

"I can't," I said. "I…"

"Do it, and be rewarded. Live the good life, like us."

"Good life?" I pointed at the bone mulch. "This is the good life?"

"Our obedience is rewarded with kindness."

Shaking my head, I walked backward, not tearing my eyes away from Ms. Needlemire's frail form. I saw the coffee mug lift toward her mouth, heard the soft slurping sounds of her drinking. My feet nearly slipped out from under me when I staggered into the ditch at the verge of her yard. I found my balance when I reached the road.

Then I ran home.

The following week, I worked alone as I tried everything possible to get us out of this house. The three-day Right to Cancel policy had expired long ago. A phone call to my lawyer offered me no help, either. I could put the house up for sale, but we didn't have enough money in the bank to afford another purchase. So I looked into rentals.

Monica was no help. She was against going back to an apartment. No house satisfied her, not even on a temporary basis. She said none of them compared to our house in Golden Gates. We'd found our home and she wouldn't leave it.

She'd tasted happiness and didn't want to lose it, no matter what.

I looked less and less for a way out. The neighbors mostly avoided us. But if we were outside as somebody walked past, they were kind and waved. Monica and I waved back, smiling.

By the third week, I no longer tried. Monica stopped speaking to me unless it was to remind me of the tithe. I buried myself in the new book, finishing up the revisions and sending the manuscript off to my pre-readers for input. While I waited to hear back, I began working on notes for the next one.

I saw Monica less and less. She avoided me like the neighbors had been. I figured she was still mad at me for trying to make us leave, and decided to let her have some space. When she was ready to let it go, she'd tell me.

On the fourth week, I began writing the new book. I'd almost made myself forget about that night last month. It seemed like a dream I'd had years ago. I could still envision the images of the nasty stains in the yards, but they were faint photographs in my memory.

Ms. Needlemire didn't pay a visit on the third Saturday of the month. I hadn't expected her to. She'd said all she needed to say.

On Sunday night, I rushed out to pick up some pizza since Monica hadn't cooked anything in a month. By the time I got back to the house, it was dark. I couldn't find Monica anywhere. After a quick search through the house, I finally located her on the back porch. She sat in the chair I usually occupied when I smoked cigars. A cigarette was pinched between her fingers. Seeing she'd started back smoking wasn't shocking. She'd quit seven times in the last three years.

"Where'd you go?" she asked without looking back.

"I got pizza. It's in the kitchen."

"Did you get our…tithe?"

"What do you think?"

I saw Monica's shoulders lift and drop with a sigh. "You know what's going to happen if we don't tithe."

"Nothing's going to happen."

"I heard Ms. Needlemire talking to you last month. I heard what she said."

"That's fine. It wasn't a big secret."

"You tried to keep it from me like a secret."

"Not really. I just didn't want…"

"Just didn't want to scare me. Yeah, I figured that." Another sigh. "Damn it, Adam. Why didn't you just get the tithe?"

"You really wanted me to?" No response. "You saw the envelope. Saw what was in it. A child. Where the hell am I supposed to find a child?"

"There're plenty out there…"

"Listen to yourself. You want me to abduct…?"

"A real husband would've handled it. He didn't have to like it, but he would've done it for his wife, for his home." Monica stabbed the cigarette in the ash tray. "We can't move, Adam. This is our home. We've worked too hard to get here to lose it now."

"We're not putting a child out there for…"

"The Chomper."

"Don't even say its name." I shivered. "It's sick. These people are sick. We shouldn't have ever moved here."

"Where else would we have found a place like this?"

"Plenty of others we liked."

"But we *chose* this one. More than that, it chose us."

"Jesus Christ. Now you sound like Ms. Needlemire."

Monica stood up, turned around to face me. Her hair hung in disheveled tangles around her face. She still had on what she'd slept in: plaid shorts and a white tank top. Barefoot, she started walking toward me. "I heard what Ms. Needlemire said."

"You already told me that."

"She said we could choose our own tithe…for forgiveness." Monica's eyes looked wild and haunted.

"Are you all right?" I asked.

"I haven't slept in days," she said. "I've been thinking about it, over and over and over. We've gone through a lot together. It was always us, a team pushing through it. But now…this place—I'm not leaving it behind for you. You can't make me."

"We won't leave," I said. I didn't realize I'd been backing up until my back hit the sliding door. "We'll make it work here."

"It's going to work," she said. Her shoulder dipped, arm lowering. I saw the bat leaning against the house. Her hand closed around its taped handle. "As always, leave it to me to fix your mess!"

I dodged her first swing. The bat smashed through the glass behind me, throwing shards onto the kitchen floor. Looking at Monica, I saw her leer. "Shit, Mon! What the hell…?"

A wicked grin splitting her face, she twirled. The bat whacked my shoulder, blasting my arm with pain before it went numb. I tried lifting it. Couldn't. It hung useless and limp beside me. So when she swung again, I had no way to protect myself. My other arm wouldn't make it in time to thwart the blow.

The bat came at my face, filling my vision.

Pain exploded in my head.

Then darkness covered everything.

Opening my eyes, I saw the night sky above me, the stars smeared in my distorted vision. My head throbbed each time I blinked. My eyelids felt as if they had weights pushing them down. There was a lot of pressure on my forehead, as if a brick had been pushed under my skin.

I couldn't move my arms. The left one felt sore and tight, but at least it was no longer numb. Didn't help matters, though. My wrists had been tied to stakes, forcing my arms straight out on each side. Looking down my chest, I saw my legs were spread, trails of rope leading from my ankles to another pair of stakes.

I'd been splayed like an X on the ground.

Looking around, I cried "Monica!" when I spotted her standing off to the side of me. The porch light painted half her face in a pale glow, leaving the other half veiled in shadow. But I saw enough of her eyes to see the hate she was throwing at me.

I felt my testicles shrink back as if trying to hide. "What are you doing?" I asked.

"Giving the Chomper what it wants."

"And that's me?"

Monica nodded. "You didn't leave me much of a choice."

"There were plenty of choices!"

"You're wrong."

Shaking my head, I said, "You'd rather offer *me* to this thing than move?"

"We'll never find a better place, a safer place."

"Monica, don't do this, okay? I'll go find our tithe. I'll do it right. I'll…"

"It's too late. Where will you find a child this time of night? Besides, I've grown to accept my decision. And if I don't give the Chomper something tonight, we're both dead. You know it. I know it. So…it has to be you."

"I would've never done this to you. I can't believe you're doing this…"

I knew I should've been enraged, but I just felt blank inside, a numbness that seemed to spread all through me. I suppose anger was in there too, but muted by my broken heart.

Monica's betrayal had left me paralyzed.

I heard the clacking of heavy heals on asphalt. Looking toward the road, I spotted Ms. Needlemire approaching. Some of the neighbors walked with her, a congregation of senior citizens moving in a lethargic wave. All of them were dressed as if they were about to go to church.

Monica noticed them, and smiled. "Ms. Needlemire, look." She pointed at me. "Here's my tithe. Will the Chomper accept it?"

Looming above me, Ms. Needlemire's mouth was a tight line that caused her wrinkles to excavate. She nodded. "Oh, yes," she said. "The Chomper will be very pleased."

Monica looked on the verge of maniacal laughter. "Oh, thank goodness. I love it here. I understand why you do this—you don't want to leave, either. And like you, I want to spend the rest of my life here."

My eyes locked on Ms. Needlemire's. They looked sympathetic behind the thick glass. "Well, Mr. Schaffer, did you expect to find yourself in this predicament?"

I tugged at the ropes. The stakes didn't budge. The rope was too tight, looped many times around my wrists. Giving up, I let my head drop on the damp ground. It soaked my hair. "No…"

Ms. Needlemire nodded. "I bet not." She looked at Monica. "We like having you here, Mrs. Schaffer. A lot. We really wish things would've been different."

"Me too," said Monica. "But I couldn't think of any other way."

"Why didn't you just do the tithe?" Ms. Needlemire asked me.

I thought about giving her some kind of snarky remark, one last jib to go out on. I had nothing. "Somebody shouldn't have to die so I can have happiness."

Ms. Needlemire stared at me. The corner of her mouth arced. "Good answer, Mr. Schaffer. I knew I liked you for a reason. That's why you got my vote."

Confused, I watched Ms. Needlemire walk toward Monica.

"Mrs. Schaffer, Golden Gates is a community for families—husbands and wives, kids. The kids grow up, move out, and the parents stay here, grow old and die. Then we are laid out on our lawns, and devoured by the Chomper. Then our children come back, take our places, keeping the cycle alive. That's our duty. In the meantime, we offer tithes to the Chomper to keep us safe, to keep our lawns looking plush, and to keep the vermin away, human and animal. Strict rules are applied here. Laws, curfews, bedtimes, all put into place to protect us. You got this opportunity because cancer took the Johnsons' only son. The house was left vacant when they were offered to the Chomper at the end of their lifespan."

"Yes," said Monica. "And I'm happy to be a part of it."

"I admire that," said Ms. Needlemire. "But what I admire more is a husband willing to fight for what he knows in his heart is right, even if it might cost him his life. We want you here, Mrs. Schaffer. But we can't stand having a selfish wife who's this quick to betray her husband to help herself."

Monica's mouth slowly dropped.

"Hold her," said Ms. Needlemire.

Before Monica could react, The Duggins' rushed her, grabbing her arms.

Pointing at me, Ms. Needlemire said, "Untie him, quickly. The Chomper's coming."

In the distance, I detected the faint rumble of an old engine, steadily growing louder. It would be here within minutes.

Mr. and Mrs. Dooley quickly untied my hands and feet. They helped me stand up. My legs tingled as if sand flowed through my veins.

"Put her in his place," said Ms. Needlemire.

"No!" Monica screamed. The older couple pulled her, thrashing and bucking, toward the ropes. "Adam! Don't let them do this! I'm sorry! I love you!"

I almost helped her, but a quick look at Ms. Needlemire convinced me to stay where I was. Monica fought and screamed, bucked and struggled, unable to get free. The Dooleys held her down while The Moores tied her.

Ms. Needlemire stepped in front of me, putting her hand against my chest. She shoved me back. "Now get inside, Mr. Schaffer. The offering has been left."

"But…" I looked at Monica, who peered up at me with tear-soaked eyes. Her lips quivered. "I…"

"Now, Mr. Schaffer. The Chomper is almost here. If we're out here when it arrives…"

She let the cautionary look in her eyes finish for her.

"Adam!" Monica cried. "Please! I'm sorry! Please, help! Adam!"

"Go," said Ms. Needlemire.

Nodding, I walked backward. Seeing me go caused Monica to shriek. It was hard to understand what she was saying through her hysterical crying. Hearing the pitiful hopelessness in her voice made my chest tighten. Tears filled my eyes.

I put my back to her and went inside. I gave one last look out. My neighbors were heading home while Monica screamed, body jerking against the ropes. She cussed them, cussed me. Then she begged for forgiveness.

I closed the door.

Within minutes I was in my bedroom, the lights out, on my knees in front of the window, gazing down into my dark front yard. Though I couldn't see Monica, I could surely hear her frantic pleas. But they were drowned out by the broken chugging of an impending engine.

Chills scurried up my spine when a bright light suddenly appeared like a glowing explosion, exposing Monica. No longer fighting, she still screamed as the light grew, spreading around her like garish water.

Then I saw the blades, twirling in a blur of sharp points. Huge, jagged teeth, spinning like the spokes of a bicycle wheel. The machine the churning fins were affixed to appeared below me. Its blocky design was shaped like a tractor, but larger, bulkier. Scarier. Smokestacks on each side pumped thick plumes of exhaust as its movements squeaked and chirped like a bad fan belt. Its design was simple, yet palpably supernatural. There was no driver. The metal beast moved by its own accord.

Monica screamed one last time before her head was munched, killing her cries with juicy crunching sounds. I looked away as the blades chewed their way to her breasts.

Getting in bed, I thought about nothing. My mind was a void, flat and empty. I didn't think I'd be able to sleep, but when my head touched the pillow, I plummeted into a deep slumber.

I didn't wake until morning, to the peaceful harmony of chimes.

Ms. Needlemire smiled when I opened the door. "Mr. Schaffer, you look well-rested."

Squinting against the bright light, I nodded. "I feel it, actually."

"See how good tithing makes you feel?"

"For now." My eyes drifted toward the yard. Where Monica had been was a trodden patch of dark wetness. Even the stakes were gone. "But I imagine the guilt will come when I have a chance to think about it."

Ms. Needlemire shook her head. "No. Your conscience is clean, nothing to punish yourself over."

"I gave my wife to a mysterious junk-heap called the Chomper. I have plenty to feel bad about."

"Not at all," she said. "Don't you feel…good?"

I'd never felt better in all my life. Lighter on my feet, I fought the urge to whistle. Where Monica had hit me with the bat no longer throbbed. Checking my arm, I saw there wasn't even a tiny blemish left behind.

"So I have to do this every month now?" I asked.

Ms. Needlemire smiled. "The blood offering is obligatory, yes. But you proved to all of us that you belong, proved it to the Chomper too. A man who'd be willing to give a child's life to help his own is not the kind of person we'd want living here in Golden Gates."

"So that was just a test?"

Ms. Needlemire's smile stretched wider. "And you passed." She held up an envelope that looked identical to the other one. "This is for you. Look at it when you get inside."

I took the envelope from her, then Ms. Needlemire turned and started her slow shuffle down my steps. "Have a good day," I told her.

"You too, Mr. Schaffer."

I started to close the door.

"Oh, one more thing," she said, turning around.

Looking out, I said, "What's that?"

"I'm having a gathering at my house next Saturday. I'd love for you to be there."

I smiled. "Wouldn't miss it."

"Good. My granddaughter's coming to stay with me for a while. She's about your age, recently divorced and very easy on the eyes. It's getting close to time for me to be offered, so she's going to help me along until then. I think you two will hit it off splendidly."

"Sounds good to me."

"Take care," she said, turning away.

I shut the door. On my way to my office, I opened the envelope. It hadn't been sealed. Inside was a single sheet of paper, folded. Opening it, I stared at the crudely drawn image.

And smiled.

In blue, smeary ink was the unmistakable likeness of a chicken.

Now that was a tithe I could handle.

Story Notes:

The original version of this story was written years back, but I tossed out most of it while rewriting it for Jack Bantry's *Splatterpunk Magazine*. I kept the wife's name the same, but changed the husband's because they matched a couple I'd come to know since completing the first draft. I didn't want them to think I'd purposely used their names, especially after what happens to them in the story.

I'm a fan of old anthology shows like *Twilight Zone, Monsters, Tales from the Darkside, and Outer Limits*. As a kid, I used to watch them with my mother, the lights turned off and drinking chocolate milkshakes while my father worked the late shift.

When I first sat down to attempt this story, I wanted to write something that I might have watched with mother back then. I'd planned to let her read it, but she never got to before dementia took hold of her. I hope she would've liked it.

LOVE SEAT

I see ya eyein' her," the old man said. "I'll sell her to ya for ten bucks." He spat a wad of brown phlegm onto the concrete.

The old man was dressed in a tan colored shirt, long-sleeved although it was nearly a hundred degrees, with a rolled pack of chewing tobacco in the chest pocket, and pants an even darker shade of brown. His gut wilted over his belt, dimpling the fabric around the buttons on his shirt.

Jacob Carlson had been at the Hickory Grove flea market for two hours, and his shirt was sodden with sweat. His mother had told him if he wanted a good deal on a couch, he should try the flea market.

You can find good stuff there. Cheap!

Until coming across this booth, he hadn't found anything nice *or* cheap. A foul-mouthed Mexican was selling some furniture still in its plastic off the back of a truck, but his prices were absurdly high, and he wouldn't haggle.

Jacob was contemplating a trip to Goodwill when he stumbled across this couch: a two-seater, red violet in color, with a high back and heavily bolstered arms that looked as soft as marshmallows. It had to be a used furnishing, or the popularly coined term 'Previously Owned' but when Jacob glided his hand across the back cushion it felt too soft, too warm, for someone to have soiled it.

"You like her, dontcha?" The man wiped his mouth, coughed, but didn't hock any odd colored mucus this time. "She's something special. You'll never find a couch like her."

There, he'd done it again, referred to the couch as *her*.

"Why are you willing to sell her—*it*—so cheap?"

The man smiled. "Because she chose you, that's why." He rubbed his hands together. "I was packing up, 'bout to head home for the day when I heard her calling. She told me the *one* had finally come to claim her."

Jacob restrained a shiver. The man might not look it, but he was quite a salesman, albeit a creepy one.

"But before I can rightfully give her up, I have to ask *you* some questions."

"Wuh-what kind of questions?" Jacob hadn't realized there would be a background screening just to buy a damn couch. But looking at its ample cushions, he could almost understand why there was. She was too lovely to be handed off to just anybody, and he could accept that.

"Why are you in the market for a new couch?"

Frowning, Jacob looked up as if the reason hovered above him. And for a couple weeks everything had felt that way, like a black fog following him everywhere. Why *did* he need a new couch? He couldn't remember. Trying to recall it was like looking through a frosted window. Something had happened, recently, and that was why he'd spent most of his Saturday off shopping for furniture. But his mind couldn't quite grasp what it was. It was painful, that much he could remember, and nasty and bitter.

Hannah.

Then the memory crashed down on him, so heavy on his shoulders he began to slouch.

He remembered it all.

He'd come home from PC Problems, where he worked, early, to avoid overtime and found a foreign, yet vaguely familiar Mazda parked in the driveway of the two-bedroom house he shared with his fiancé, Hannah. The car sat in the spot where he normally parked *his* car. And because the short narrow driveway was occupied by Hannah's Jetta and this Mazda, Jacob was forced to park at the curb. On Mable Street, he could do that without having to worry someone would bust his windows and steal something.

Plus, with him parking at the curb, Hannah hadn't heard his arrival.

"Son?"

Jacob fluttered his eyes, shook his head to knock the cobwebs loose. "Yuh-yeah?"

"You just kind of zoned out there." The man brandished a handkerchief from a rear pocket that had probably been white when it came out of the package, now it was forever yellowed. Then he wiped his brow, running the kerchief over his bald dome, and the horseshoe of hair around it.

"Sorry…I was …Never mind."

"So, you were about to answer my question?"

Was he? Right. The question that had triggered the unwanted recollection. "My fiancé and I are separating…I moved into an apartment. It wasn't furnished."

"Ah. Okay. So you're single."

"Well, sort of…at the moment, yeah, but I don't know how long this will be going on. But for now, yeah, I guess you can say I am."

"Good." He wiped his hands, then put the dirty square back in his pocket. "She isn't going home with someone that's already taken. This couch is special, and not meant to be shared. Know what I mean?"

"No…actually I have no idea."

Ignoring him, the man delicately patted the couch. "She's not just something you plop your ass down on at the end of the day. This couch is so much more. You take her home and you are committing yourself to her. Your life will never be the same. Can you do that—uh, what's your name, son?"

"Jacob."

"Can you do that, Jacob? Can you give all of yourself to such an immaculate piece of furniture?"

This old man was beginning to really bother Jacob, speaking like a father would about his daughter before allowing her to leave the house on prom night. He was ready to tell this guy thanks but no thanks, when his mind went fuzzy again. All the negative thoughts, the second guesses began to dissolve, and in their place came comfort. Tranquility. These were feelings he wasn't used to, not since he was a child on his mother's lap being rocked to sleep. He'd felt so safe then, so loved, and was feeling that way now.

Jacob rubbed the couch again, the downy material soft and plushy against his hand. He found himself wanting to squeeze it.

"Can't keep letting ya grope her if you don't plan on buyin' her."

"Ten bucks?"

"From you I'll take five. Like I said, she wants to go home with *you*, and she's a tough one to please."

"I'll take her." This time, Jacob didn't even notice—or care—he'd started referring to the couch in the flesh and blood sense as well.

"You won't regret this."

"Thank you, mister…I don't even know *your* name."

"Just call me Gus."

"Thank you, Gus, for all your help."

"Don't thank me, thank her." He nodded at the couch.

Jacob silently did.

Gus told him to pull around to the back and take the gravel road that circled around the hive-like buildings. Then he shook the old man's hand, and went out to his truck. When he got back there, Gus already had the couch's body wrapped in plastic. He'd removed the seat cushions and placed them in padded bags.

The old man waved at Jacob as he parked the truck. "I haven't seen her so excited in a *long* time. I think she'd 'bout given up hope the right one would come along and take her home."

For some reason, Jacob felt himself beginning to blush.

On his way home, he went through the Burger King drive-thru, got a double cheeseburger combo, and ate it as he drove. Every so often, he checked the rearview mirror where he could see the loveseat in the bed of his truck. Afraid of going too fast and the cushions blowing away, he made sure to keep the speed five miles below the required limit.

He had finished eating and was sipping on his Coke when he pulled into the driveway. Jacob's abode was considered an apartment, although it had been a house at one time—a very old house, and had been converted into two separate apartments, upstairs and down. Nobody lived above him, and the landlord had told him it would probably remain vacant since he'd gotten too old to go up and down those stairs himself. Jacob was just fine with that. The idea of having someone trampling all over his ceiling at odd hours didn't sound very appealing.

He dropped his trash in the can outside, then walked over to the tailgate, and lowered it. He studied the couch through the plastic wrap. Its design was so basic, yet incomparable to anything he'd ever seen, the kind of furniture Jacob wouldn't normally want to own. But from the first glance, he knew this couch wasn't an ordinary furnishing. Something about her was otherworldly.

She chose you. And she's a tough one to please.

Jacob smiled, feeling good about that.

Two hours later he had the couch in the living room, unwrapped, and on display. He stood there, gazing at her proudly. She was an article of exuberance, much too beautiful for this shitty place Jacob was renting for two-hundred dollars a month.

He wondered what Hannah would think of her, then realized he didn't really care what she would've thought.

A couch like this isn't meant to be shared...

He hadn't sat on her yet. Her sloping softness beckoned him. But he was sweaty, and his clothes were filthy. He decided to shower first.

Standing under the hot streams, his mind wandered to six weeks ago, as it often did when he was alone. He was standing on the front porch, his key to the doorknob of the house he shared with Hannah, about to put the key in when a faint noise resonated from deep inside.

A throaty gasp.

Hannah.

Jacob didn't kick down the door and rush to her rescue. It wasn't that kind of gasp. It was the kind Hannah used during certain secretive pleasures, like the time he'd accidentally walked in on her with an immense dildo to the hilt between her legs as she lay sweaty and mussed on the bed. The whole room had reeked of dirty sex.

Could she be in there pleasuring herself again?

It had been more awkward for *him* the last time than for her. It had also put an idea in the hind regions of his mind that he wasn't enough to satisfy the urges she obviously had, but was too ashamed to discuss with him. Perhaps it was because when it came to sex, Jacob didn't color outside the lines. He was a simple, three position man and didn't much care for trying new things. He hadn't even watched a porno since he was a teenager, yet adult sites kept popping up in his internet browser's history. He figured that was Hannah's doing as well, though he'd never confronted her about it.

As he'd put the key in the lock, Hannah cried out. "Fuck me…Yeah…Yeah…"

He froze.

His heart hammered against his chest. Something cold and prickly rose up into his throat. He began to shiver in the late May heat.

"Stick it in my ass! You want to, don't you? Fuck my ass…"

Jacob's eyes swelled. He looked over at the Mazda, knowing that he would not be interrupting a masturbation session. This time she had a partner.

Delicately, he turned the key, disengaging the deadbolt. Then he curled his fingers around the knob. It felt cold and clammy in his hand. He opened the door and was slapped in the face with a domineering odor.

The musky scent of sex.

Hannah's moans and cries were much louder now. He eased the door shut, hoping to stifle the clicking of the latch. He probably could've kicked the door shut and it wouldn't have registered above Hannah's sounds.

"Oh my God…fuck yeah…I think I'm gonna come…"

Tears spilled from Jacob's eyes as he staggered across the living room on his way to the kitchen, using legs that felt too weak and stringy to carry him. His head spun. Everything brightened as if he was in a really bad dream.

"I'm so close…" she rasped.

Jacob bit down on his lip as he stepped up to the kitchen doorway. Hannah sat naked on the edge of the table where they had eaten many meals together, this very morning in fact, leaned back on her elbows, her legs spread. Her skin was slick with sweat. Each foot was arched, toes down on a separate chair for leverage. Head leaned back, her breasts heaved. Strands of hair were glued to her shoulders from sweat. The dildo was inside of her, but instead of her groin, it was up to the hilt in her ass—vigorously going in and out.

He'd been right. She wasn't alone. She had a partner who was also naked, holding the dildo, and sitting in a chair between Hannah's legs as if she were prepared to catch a baby. Her short blond hair was wavy and wet against her neck. He recognized her immediately, although his confusion as to why she was here when she was married to Hannah's brother nearly made his brain split.

He watched them for minutes that ticked by like days. Watched as Hannah's body convulsed when her orgasm ravaged her, spraying lines of juices from her sex. He'd never seen her squirt before. Another sign he wasn't enough to please her. It was a marvel the table didn't collapse underneath her from how hard her body quaked.

Then Hannah climbed off the table.

Kissing and fondling each other, Hannah eased her sister-in-law in her place and was about to use the dildo on her before Jacob's sobs gave him away.

The heated fights, the anger and shame that shadowed them for the next several weeks had been awful. His brother-in-law threw his wife, and mother of his two children, out of the house. Last Jacob had heard, he was trying to get her parental rights taken away.

Unsuccessful at fixing things, and finally understanding that Hannah didn't really want them to be fixed, Jacob moved out. And *Jennifer*, Hannah's ex-sister-in-law, moved in.

The shower no longer sprayed warm water on him, but cold. He wasn't sure how long he'd been standing there in his abandoned state, but it had been long enough to waste all of the hot water. It felt like arctic needles nicking his skin. He quickly turned off the water, climbed out, and blanketed himself with a towel. He stood on the bathmat, shivering, feeling the humiliation all over again as if he were experiencing it presently.

Then he heard it, supple and pleasing, resonating all around him.

Come to me.

The sadness, the shame, all of it lifted. All that remained was her.

He could see her in the living room. Waiting. Beckoning. Wanting. Her squishy padding, the dark red color, called to him. He wanted to feel it against his skin. He let the towel drop to his ankles, his erection pointing rigid ahead of him.

He left the bathroom. It felt as if he was walking on cotton. He'd never just lounged naked before, not when he'd lived with Hannah, and definitely not before or since.

And it felt good, elating.

It felt as if he were underwater, the bubbling in his ears, a thickness pressing against his throat. His steps were heavy and sluggish. He could hardly breathe as he approached her, running his hand along her arm. Sliding sinuously against her, he never once thought it odd, or dirty that he was rubbing his naked body against his couch like a cat against someone's leg. It felt right gliding his hands across the velvety cushions, massaging them, burying his face between them and flicking their creases with his tongue.

He sat down on the floor in front of the loveseat, crossed his legs, and leaned forward, putting his tongue where the cushions met in the front and made a hole. He tingled as if he'd just licked a battery. Through the deluge in his ears, he could hear soft, whispery moans.

Yes…Oooh…I like that…

He put a hand on each cushion, pushed his thumbs together and folded the cushions back, exposing the tab of a small zipper. Shiny and glossy, it beckoned him. He leaned forward, tapping it with the tip of his tongue, sucking it in and flicking it again and again. The moans in his ears became throaty cries that begged him to continue, not to stop, because she was getting so close…so close…

He pushed his index finger into the hole and felt the cushions quiver. He rotated it this way and that, drenching his finger with the fluids seeping from the fabric. The steady gasps in his ears rose to a fever-pitch, his head pounding, then it all released, sousing his mouth and chin in a syrupy thickness, warm and salty with a vague taste of cotton. The loveseat trembled, its wooden frame knocking against the wall as it continued to saturate him.

I need you inside me Jacob. I need you, now.

He sat back, backhanded the lather from his lips, and got on his knees. His hard-on pulsated, throbbing so much it hurt. He gripped the shaft below the engorged head, scooting forward on his knees.

Then he pushed himself into the hole.

The soggy cushions hugged him firmly, taking him all the way inside. She sheathed his penis with moist padding. He began to thrust, delicate and slow at first, but his rhythm increased as did his need. He gripped the arms of the couch as if they were her hands and squeezed as he slammed into her. The loveseat banged against the wall, scratching a straight-line in the paint.

Jacob could faintly hear growling, and when he realized it was coming from his own throat, he began to howl. The loveseat continued instructing him, demanding him to go harder and faster, to take out his aggressions on her, to prove to himself that he was good at what he did. He needed to open himself up, allow who he was on the inside to come out and play. There was no shame, no humiliation, because he could be himself with her. He could let her see who he truly was.

Jacob didn't have to hide from her.

He felt his climax pushing through his veins, swelling his penis.

Then he erupted, spurting thick gloppy puddles inside of her. His growls bellowed as he quaked. He continued to thrust as he emptied himself inside the pleat between the cushions.

He fell over her, panting, his head buried against the back stuffing. His throat was scratchy and dry, his lips parched. He let a few moments pass to catch his breath, then pulled out of her. Glistening, red fibers clung to the stickiness that coated his penis.

Sitting back on his knees, Jacob ran a hand through his soaked hair. He closed his eyes, leaned back his head. He could feel the smile on his face. The love seat made him feel as if he could do nothing to disappoint her.

And you couldn't...

The voice was soft, raspy in his mind, and just as winded as he. Smiling, he climbed up on the couch, curled up, and went to sleep.

He didn't wake up until morning.

Jacob could not remember ever feeling so good...so *refreshed*. Whistling, he went to the toilet to empty his bladder. His pee sputtered as it came out, the aftereffect of a good orgasm. When he was finished, he went back to the living room and made love to the loveseat again.

Then he cooked a breakfast of scrambled eggs and bacon and ate it on the couch while flipping through channels on TV. He settled for a giant reptile movie on *Syfy*. It was awful, but cheesy enough that it held his interest. When his plate was clean, he sat it on the end table, had sex with the couch again, and then took a nap on her comfy cushions.

He dreamed. There was nothing to see, just total blackness, but the soft voice was there with him in the dark. When she spoke, a purple orb flickered with each syllable, illuminating only briefly the vast expanse of emptiness where it was just the two of them.

I have to feed.

"What should I feed you?"

Think about it...You know what I need to live...to be with you, to satisfy you.

He didn't have to think about it. Somehow, he already knew exactly what it was that she must consume in order to remain his.

I will begin to abrade, and my seat will no longer be soft. Inside, I will dry up, become brittle and coarse. My skin will tear, rip, and become too stale. I will not be able to satisfy you, and you will grow tired of me.

"I would never be tired of you."

You will...

"Then what should I do?"

You already know what you should do...

****

He awoke on the couch with an icy block between his shoulders. He looked at the clock hanging above the mantel. It was almost three. He'd nearly slept through the whole day. But being Sunday, the flea market would be open for two more hours.

He hoped the old man was there.

He needed to talk to him.

The Pine Grove Flea Market was practically deserted. The few people browsing were like lost souls wandering between two worlds in a daze. The cheerless, worn expressions on their faces were open books to a private life of pain and misery. Had he looked like that yesterday? Probably. Wait, not yesterday...that had to have been days ago. But it wasn't.

He hurried to the building where the old man's shop had been. Walking so fast, he was virtually running as he approached the lot number. It was vacant. The shelves that had displayed various knick-knacks were empty. A blue tarp covered a card table to the left. It lay flat upon it. No shapes or objects hidden underneath.

Shit.

He turned around, scanning the building up one side and down the other from where he stood. No sign of Gus.

Then he heard a rusted crank behind him. He whirled around, catching Gus raising the metal door on his way in. Two boxes sat on the concrete, both taped shut. He'd obviously been returning to fetch them. He glanced at Jacob, nodded, and then went to grab the boxes, but stopped. He looked back, recognition kicking in.

"I'd almost given up on you."

Jacob stepped as close as the counter would allow. "You remember me?"

"Of course I do, it was only yesterday when you were here."

Jacob swallowed. It was wet and bubbly. "I think you probably know why I'm here."

Gus nodded, the corner of his mouth twitching as if it were attempting a smile. "I'm sure I do."

"Tell me this…Is what I'm thinking true?"

"She told you she needed to feed?" Jacob nodded. "Then what you're thinking is *exactly* true. I told you, there wasn't a couch like her."

"She isn't just a couch. She's more."

"And so what if she is?" Gus spat. It popped when it hit the floor. "I can tell just by looking in your eyes that you are happier than you've been in a long time. Hell, probably ever. Am *I* right about that?"

Jacob could've lied, but Gus would have seen through it.

"That's what I thought," said Gus. Squatting, he scooped up a box, pressing it against his chest as he stood. Then he sat it on the tarp-covered table. "Listen, you know what they say: In order for true happiness, you have to make some sacrifices…and that's accurate."

Sacrifices.

Ice flowed through Jacob's veins. He shuddered. "I know what she's telling me…I just don't think I can…"

Gus smirked. "I know exactly how you feel." He waved his hand toward him. "Might as well come outside and have a seat. I've got a cooler back there with some Dr. Pepper in it. Want one?"

Jacob hadn't realized just how thirsty he was until Gus mentioned it. "Yes, that would be great."

"Thought so. You have to keep your body hydrated and healthy for her. I recommend drinking a lot of water and milk…"

Jacob stepped around the counter, following Gus through the opened garage door. Behind the building, Gus's moving truck was backed up to the door with its rear gate raised. A cooler sat at the edge of the cargo bay, a folding chair on each side. Jacob looked at Gus, a confused expression on his face, but before he could ask, Gus nodded.

"I thought you might come by."

Gus grabbed the handle and hoisted himself up. Jacob took the ramp. They each sat in a chair. As Gus opened the cooler and fished through the ice for two cans of Dr. Pepper, Jacob leaned forward, drumming his fingers together. He stopped when Gus passed him a can. "Here ya go, nice and cold."

The can was frosty and wet in his hand. He popped the tab and took a long, hard swallow. The drink burned, but was refreshing as it decanted down his throat. "If you knew I would come by, then why didn't you just tell me all of this yesterday?"

Gus drank before answering. "Would you have taken her if I had?"

"Of course not."

"And that's why I didn't tell you yesterday." Gus drank some more before continuing. "You were meant to have her. If I would've said something about it then you would have said no right away, and I couldn't stand in the way of that."

"But you could profit."

"You call five bucks a profit?" Gus croaked a laugh. "Please." He took another sip. "It wasn't even enough to cover this soda and ice."

"Glad I could help."

Gus's deep-south drawl took on a more intelligent quality. "Listen, you can do what she needs, or you can ignore it. But I'll tell you this much—if you ignore it, you'll find yourself worse than you were before she came along. Your health will dwindle; your looks will go bad. I lost weight, couldn't stop sweating, my eyes looked like they were sucking into my head. You'll lose your hair, and your teeth'll start falling out. See?" Gus reached into his mouth, pinched his front teeth between his forefinger and thumb, then pulled them from his mouth. Dentures. In his hand was a perfect set of artificial teeth. "Happened to me."

"Wait…you mean…her…"

Gus nodded. "Yep. Basically, if you give up on her, you give up on yourself. She was mine for twenty years. I came across her four months after my wife Mary was raped and murdered. I tried to kill myself, but fucked it up, so I ended up spending some time in a hospital." He tapped a finger against his temple. "A *mental* hospital."

"Jesus."

"So when they thought I was *fit* to give life another go, they let me out. I went back home, trying to piece together what was left of the wreck my life had become since losing Mary. One thing I had to do was get rid of all the furniture that she had put in our house, which was damn near everything. Seeing it all the time was just too much. So I got this truck here," he patted the sidewall, "and loaded it up. I took the furniture to a thrift store and donated it. The lady who owned the place was so thankful for what I had done, but she also worried about what *I* would sit on, and with my Mary dead and gone, who'd keep me company.

I tried convincing her I'd be all right, but she didn't believe it. Hell, I didn't believe it myself. So she took me into the back where she kept what she called the *special* items and took me straight to the loveseat. God, I can still remember how she just seemed to glow in that dark room. Everything else was junk compared to her. It almost seemed like a light was shining down from Heaven on her just to make sure I didn't overlook her."

"So you took her home?"

"Yep. For two bucks." He winked. "And she made me happy for the first couple days. Then she told me she needed to feed."

Another flurry of spider legs scurried up Jacob's back.

Feed.

"And to feed her...I mean...what she eats is...is..."

"Blood." Jacob closed his eyes, leaned back his head. "Shit."

"You better believe it." Gus swigged from the can, emptying it. He crushed it in his palm, and tossed it behind him. Fishing through the cooler for another, he continued, "She's not picky, either. Hell, she'll take the whole thing." He sat up, popped the tab. It was like a shotgun blast in the tight compartment. "You know what I mean by the *whole* thing, right?"

Jacob nodded. *The entire body.* He didn't need to ask if the blood had to be human, because somehow, he already knew it needed to be.

"The first was the hardest. That'll be the hardest for you, too. Well, the second one is no walk-in-the-park either, but it's a *tad* bit easier. By the fourth and so on, you don't hardly feel a thing anymore."

"What is she, really?"

Gus swigged some soda, shrugged. "Hell if I know. I stopped trying to figure that out and just enjoyed it. But for me to be happy, and for *you* to be happy now, you have to keep *her* happy."

Jacob thought he might get sick. The Dr. Pepper that had been so cool and wonderful just minutes ago sat on his stomach like tainted water. "I don't think I can."

"Well, if you want her, you'll have to. And believe me, if you give up on her, you'll regret it until you die. When I tried to avoid *feeding* her for a stretch it felt like *I* was the one dying. I was like a drug addict that needed a fix or something. I was just so weak all the time, but when I caved in and *fed* her, everything was perfect."

"If it was so perfect, then why did you sell her to me?"

"Because, Jacob, I'm an old man. I can't keep this up like I used to. But she can go on and on. She just needs the right mate to help her." Gus leaned over, patting Jacob on the back. "And I meant what I said when I told you she chose you. She could feel you coming to get her days before you even knew you would be. She's like that. Almost like magic."

Almost?

Sighing, Jacob rubbed his face with his hands. "I just don't think I can give her someone to *feed* on. I just couldn't take a human being, and…*offer*…them to her."

"Oh, sure you can. Just do what I did." He drank from the can, belched a breathy burp. "Pick someone you don't like."

"Wuh-what?"

"I'm sure there's someone that has wronged you. Just take them and offer *their* blood to the loveseat. It won't make the taking of a human life part any easier, but the guilt won't be so bad. Trust me."

After that, Jacob was quiet. Of course there was someone that had wronged him. Severely. There was always someone who had wronged *any*one, severely, but Jacob felt that his culprit was worse than most others. He wondered if he could do it, even to someone as cold-hearted and selfish as Hannah.

Only one way to find out…

He thanked Gus for his time.

"Just remember," Gus began. "It will all be worth it in the long run." Before Jacob was out of earshot, Gus added, "Don't get caught."

****

After dark, Jacob drove to Mable Street. He parked his car in the cul-de-sac, two blocks down from the house. Hopefully Hannah hadn't changed the locks yet, because he still had a spare key that she was unaware of.

Using the moon as his light, he followed its gray paths etched through the yard to the back door. Most of the lights downstairs were off, but upstairs the bedroom light glowed, a bright square amongst the blackness. He fished the key out of his pocket, put it into the lock, and twisted. There was a faint click. He smiled. He'd figured she would've been too lazy to change the locks, something he would have done without delay. But he supposed there wasn't a hurry to do so, because she probably hadn't once considered the possibility that Jacob would show up to kidnap her and offer her to a demonic loveseat.

Even as he thought it, the situation felt justified and not odd or foul.

He knew the house so well that he moved through the kitchen and up the stairs in stealth. His feet avoided the sags that would cause a squeak or pop. At the top, Jacob glanced down the hall to the master bedroom. The door was opened a crack, a bar of light shining on the carpet. He crept to the door. As he got closer, he could hear the soft sound from the TV. *Family Guy.* She loved that show. He peeked inside and saw her.

Hannah.

She lay on the bed, head propped on pillows and eating a bowl of ice cream in a t-shirt and panties. Her new lover was nowhere to be seen. He briefly wondered where she might be as he pushed the door open.

Hannah turned to him, the spoon of vanilla ice cream suspended in front of her mouth, her eyes round as spheres. "Juh-Jacob?"

Then he was on her. His hands gripped her throat, banging her head against the headboard until she no longer struggled. The ice cream had toppled over, spilling a cold, white pile on the sheets. He checked her pulse. Still breathing. He scooped her off the bed, throwing her over his shoulder and quickly fled back to his truck.

Then he was heading to the apartment he shared with the loveseat. He kept to the speed limits, singing along with the songs on the radio.

When he arrived at the apartment, he dug out a handful of the napkins he'd kept from Burger King, went around to the bed of the truck, and opened it. Hannah was awake, but dazed, and before she had the chance to scream, he stuffed the napkins in her mouth.

While she fought to spit them out, he carried her inside.

He tossed her to the floor, at the base of the loveseat.

Thank you my dear. He heard her whisper.

"Jacob? What are you doing? What is…?" But before she could finish, a sonorous roar resounded from deep inside the couch, silencing Hannah in midsentence. She turned toward the couch, then slowly back to Jacob, looking as if she wanted to ask him a question.

Jacob gasped when the cushions sprung open like a mouth. A writhing flesh-colored tentacle lapped out, slithering over the front, and finding Hannah's ankles. The snake-thing curled around them. Hannah screamed. Another tentacle shot out, penetrating her mouth. Her throat bulged as it traveled down into her stomach. She gurgled, choking on it. Then the tentacles hoisted her in the air, pulling her into the loveseat. She struggled against them, trying to break free, but her attempts were fruitless. She disappeared into the couch. The cushions closed after her darting hands went underneath.

Then the loveseat belched.

Full and satisfied.

After a moment, Jacob turned and walked away. He was surprised he felt nothing at all over what had just transpired.

He showered.

After he finished, he went to the loveseat, naked and dripping. They made love several times during the night. She introduced him to other creative techniques using her tentacles, taking him to intense heights he never thought he could reach.

Without her, he wouldn't have.

And he was her favorite of all she'd ever had. He knew for certain. He could feel it.

The next morning, needing to gather his energy for another day of adolescent-like frolicking, he called out of work. When his boss told him he had acquired more than enough paid time-off hours and he could use some of them for a mini-vacation, Jacob was ecstatic.

The honeymoon was far from over, and the loveseat wouldn't need to feed for several more days. When the time came, he would find Jennifer, and reunite her with Hannah.

After that…well, he'd already begun preparing a list of prospects.

Story Notes:
I was asked to contribute to an anthology back in 2011. This was the story I wrote. It was rejected. I sent the story over to a friend of my wife's, who'd

graduated from college as an English major with aspirations of being an editor. After reading this story, she went on to become one of my pre-readers for years to follow. She's retired from it now to raise her kids. I was surprised that she kept on helping me for as long as she did because the subject matter of my books must have rattled her a bit.

I've always been very happy with how this story turned out and wanted it to get out there. Though it's popped up here and there a few times, I wanted it to be a part of this collection.

SOMETHING'S OUT THERE?

*T*ammy didn't like how the campfire caused creepy shadows to writhe on the trees. They reminded her of snakes, which she was certain were slithering in the woods around them. Unseen. She also didn't like the way the full moon looked like a giant eye staring down at her from the black sky.

And all the noises—the crackling of leaves and snapping of sticks in the darkness outside the orange smolder of the campfire, the trilling of crickets and frogs. She hated nature. Always had since she'd gone camping with her family when she was nine. Now that she was twenty-five, she should have outgrown such feelings.

They're worse.

"Your smore is ready," said Russ.

She looked up and saw him putting another graham cracker on top of a gloppy mound of melted marshmallow.

At least the food's good.

"Thanks," she muttered. Holding out her hand, she smiled.

Russ *loved* the outdoors. She wouldn't have been surprised if he confessed that he'd been raised in the deep wilderness because of the way he embraced it. When they'd settled here at this campsite after hiking all day, he'd hardly seemed winded. He'd gone and chopped plenty of wood for the night while Tammy stayed in the tent, rubbing her sore legs. Even his hair still looked great. It was parted on the side and fell across his brow, dabbing his eyebrows.

Russ frowned. It caused his handsome face to crinkle and look older. "Something bothering you?" He placed her smore in her hand.

"Well…"

A screech ripped through the night.

Squealing, Tammy dropped her smore. It broke apart on the ground.

"*Shit!*"

Russ laughed. "It was just an owl, babe."

"No owl I've ever heard."

Nodding, Russ said, "It just caught its food for the night."

"Great. And caused me to drop *mine*."

"I'll make you another."

Tammy sighed. "Thanks."

Russ removed a pane of graham from the package and placed it on his knees. He put the rest of the chocolate bar on the graham. Then he stabbed two marshmallows on the poker and lowered them into the fire. "You really hate it out here, don't you?"

"I just feel about the outdoors the way you seem to feel about hotels."

"Oh, boy. Don't start." He raised the poker. The tip was flapping with fire. He blew it out. The marshmallows were crispy and brown, just the way Tammy liked them.

"Start what? I'm serious."

"What's the point of going to the mountains if you're going to stay in a hotel? You do that at the beach, not out here."

"It's more comfortable."

"Depends on who you ask."

"Not as many animals or…" A moth flew in front of her face. She swatted at it, but missed. "Bugs."

"Depends on the hotel."

Tammy felt a smile tugging at the corners of her mouth. "And safer."

"Sometimes."

"At least we'd be behind locked doors."

"Are you still worried about those missing hikers?"

"Yes. And why aren't you?"

"Because that was months ago and not anywhere near here."

"Near enough."

Russ finished her smore and passed it over. "Eat it quick before another owl decides it wants a nighttime snack."

"Ha-ha." Tammy took a bite. The cracker crumbled in her mouth. The marshmallow was thick and gooey, but mixed with the chocolate it tasted wonderful. "Delicious."

"Now I can eat one."

While Tammy ate her gloppy treat, Russ prepared his. She felt kind of bad for not waiting for him.

He took a bite of his and moaned. Chewing, he said, "So if we're not staying in a hotel, does that mean I shouldn't try being romantic tonight."

Tammy snorted. "Do you know how sore my legs are?"

"They don't have to do anything but spread. I'll take it from there."

"How charming."

"Just wait. You'll see that woods sex is the best sex."

"Wow. I'm so into you right now, my clothes might just explode from my body."

Russ smiled. It caused dimples in his cheeks. Tammy's heart beat faster. He was good at that, making her want him even when she felt too exhausted to move. Not only was he great in bed, he was a pretty good guy too. She was lucky to have him, but she'd never tell him that. His head might expand to the point of bursting.

"If you let my animal instincts take over, I'll *ravage* you!" Russ jumped to his feet, threw back his head, and loosed a wild howl that reverberated through the night.

Scrunching her shoulders, Tammy looked around. Though she knew they were most likely alone this deep in the mountains, she still worried somebody might have heard him. "A little louder, why don't you?'

Russ laughed. "Loosen up, babe. We're in the wilderness."

"We are?" Tammy put her hand to the ground and pinched some dirt. She held it up, letting it trickle through her fingers. "I can't believe it. This *is* the wilderness. There's been a glitch in the matrix!"

Smirking, Russ stuffed the rest of the smore in his mouth. The smacks of his loud chewing almost obscured the crackling sizzle of the campfire. "You have my permission to be loud, too." His face was smudged in shadow, but she could still see him wink.

"You're a punk, you know that?"

"Yeah, I do. You need to set higher standards. Look who it got you stuck with."

"Don't remind me." She tried not to smile, but it was too hard not to.

Seeing hers, Russ smiled back. "How about we climb into the tent?"

"What about the fire?"

"It'll burn down soon enough. We won't need it anyway."

"Ohhh. Confident, huh?"

Russ shrugged. "Haven't heard any complaints."

"Yeah, well, these animal instincts better be something amazing or I'm having you neutered."

Whimpering like a hurt puppy, Russ scampered to the tent. He unzipped the flap and crawled inside.

Tammy stood, stretched. She felt a dull tug in her lower back. She really was very sore. She didn't know how she would be able to do this again tomorrow. Maybe after they were on the trail for a little while, the soreness would just go away. She doubted it, though.

She was heading to the tent when something crashed in the woods. It sounded like a tree limb had been ripped in half then tossed through the trees.

Looking at the woods, Tammy stared at pale columns of tree trunks, the thick darkness between them, and the smoke of the fire thinning as it swirled away from the campsite. She thought she heard something moving around in the black, beyond the reach of the firelight.

Then she saw a pair of glowing eyes staring at her. They blinked and were gone.

Forget this!

Tammy turned and ran to the tent. Reaching the front, she dived inside.

And landed at Russ's feet. Looking up, she huffed away the hair hanging in her face.

Naked, Russ leaned back on his elbows. His massive erection protruded between his legs like half a baseball bat. "There you are," he said. "Saved you a seat."

"Russ, really?"

"What?"

She thought about telling him what she heard, then decided against it. He would only point out again that they were in the woods, and they were apt to hear a lot of strange noises.

But the eyes.

Probably a raccoon, he'd say. Or some other kind of common forest critter.

Most likely, Tammy realized, he'd be right.

Tammy noticed Russ's penis twitch like a beckoning finger. "Come here," he said.

Forgetting about the strange sounds, Tammy crawled over to Russ. She put a hand on each side of his legs, making her way up higher. She leaned back on her knees, tugged off her shirt. The cool air licked her skin around her bra. She was reaching behind her back to unhook the straps when something crunched outside the tent.

She paused.

Russ must have noticed her hesitation. "It's fine. Don't let a little noise hold you up."

"This show is supposed to be for an audience of one."

"The forest animals like to watch, though. Kinky bastards."

Smiling, she unhooked her bra. It slid down her breasts, where she caught it and held it in front of them. Russ stuck out his bottom lip in a pretend pout. "I should make you beg for it," she said. "Putting me in the middle of the woods, forcing me to fornicate in a tent instead of a nice, comfy bed." She clucked her tongue.

"You think I'm above begging? I have no shame."

Holding her bra over her breasts with one hand, she gripped his hardness with her other. Tensing, Russ let out a quivery breath. She began to stroke.

Russ moaned.

"So didn't you have some begging to…"

A shadow raked across the tent.

Tammy jumped back, tugging Russ's penis with her. "Did you see that?" Tammy said, letting go of his softening penis. She fumbled with the straps of her bra to hook them back together. "That shadow!"

The groans that came from her boyfriend were devoid of anything pleasurable. "Y…Yeah…" said Russ, rolling onto his side. His penis was shrinking. "Probably a bear or something."

Tammy felt an icy clutch in her stomach. "Is that supposed to make me feel better?"

Holding his crotch, Russ moaned.

Realizing what she'd done, Tammy wrinkled her nose. "Sorry about that."

"Jesus," he muttered. "I think you broke it."

Heavy stomps crunched leaves outside the tent. Tammy let out a quiet gasp.

Russ turned his head, staring toward the tent flap. "All right," he said. Sitting up, he grabbed his undershorts and pulled them on. Then he put on his pants. Shirtless, he started crawling toward the front of the tent. "I'm going to take a peek outside. Will that make you feel better?"

Tammy didn't answer. She pulled her shirt on. By the time she'd tugged it straight, Russ was reaching for the zipper tab.

"Be careful!" she said in a loud voice.

Russ jerked at her voice, whipped his head around, and shushed her. Tammy mouthed her apology and watched as he slowly pulled the tab. Russ glanced back at her, wriggled his eyebrows, then stuck his head through the flap.

The vinyl sheet made whispery sounds as Russ looked this way and that.

"See anything?" whispered Tammy.

"Nope. I don't see anything except our fire. Oh, wait…"

Tammy's body stiffened. He could see something.

Russ gasped. "That can't be—"

A quick growl erupted, cut off by a whipping sound of something moving through the air. It ended with a juicy squelch. Russ's legs kicked.

"Russ?" said Tammy. Her heart pounded. She could feel it in her throat. *"Russ!"*

Twitching, Russ turned to face Tammy.

Tammy screamed when she saw the four huge gashes stretched across his face. From his hairline to his chin were ragged tears, spouting blood. His mouth was moving as he tried to talk.

Then he turned blurry from Tammy's tears, and she was thankful she could no longer see how ruined his handsome face had become.

She reached out to him. Before her fingers made it to his shoulder, Russ was yanked out of the tent. The flap swung back and forth like a doggie door.

Tammy crawled to the flap. She was about to go out for him, but Russ's screams stopped her. Growls and chomping sounds mixed with her boyfriend's cries.

Tammy zipped the flap back closed as if it might be enough to protect her. Russ continued to scream. He called for Tammy to help him. Tammy shook her head, pulled her legs to her chest.

"Please!" Russ begged.

Covering her ears with her hands, Tammy buried her face between her bare knees. It was too late to help him. She told herself over and over there was nothing she could have done.

The agonizing din faded away. Russ made a few throaty whines before going quiet. Then she heard nothing at all. Even the sounds of the forest had gone quiet, as if afraid.

Tammy raised her head, lowering her hands from her ears.

A shadow shambled across the tent. She followed it as it passed by, moved around the back and to the other side.

Circling her.

"Go away!" Tammy yelled. "Leave me alone!"

She heard a low, rattling growl as the slinking shadow moved around the front, coming back to the side.

"Get out of here!" Tammy yelled again.

Another growl. Tammy wondered if Russ had been right that it was a bear. She didn't know how it was possible. They'd taken precautions to prevent attracting one. Plus, the thing outside was walking on its hind legs. She could see its gait through the flimsy walls, the shapes of its legs—narrow and arched, walking like a man.

But it has a tail.

Its fluffy length was curled like a smirk.

The thing reached the rear of the tent and stopped. Its heavy breathing trembled against the vinyl wall.

What's it doing?

A hairy hand with elongated fingers tipped with claws ripped through the vinyl. Before Tammy could react, the tent was torn wide. A long, rigid snout pushed through the shreds, its long fangs dripping thick goops of slobber.

Yellow eyes glared in at her. She recognized them from the woods, when they'd been watching her earlier.

Tammy couldn't scream. She stared at those eyes, unable to believe what she was seeing.

It's a...

Werewolf.

It looked so much like any of the creatures she'd seen in any horror movie—a muscular, silver-haired torso and thick arms with long hair hanging from the underside like dingy tassels. As if to prove its species, it unleashed a howl that rattled Tammy's insides.

She rolled over and slapped at the tent floor while she crawled to the flap. Her palsied hands struggled to unzip the flap. Glancing over her shoulder, she saw the werewolf, hunched over, entering the tent through the shredded wall. If it got in before she could escape, she would be trapped in here with it.

Her eyes glimpsed the slug-like appendage sprouting from between its legs, a dark sheath of foreskin folding back as the pink, sliming tube expanded.

"No!"

Tammy got the flap open far enough to squeeze through. She spotted Russ's mangled corpse off to the side, his intestines splayed and scattered. His throat had been ripped out. Then she was on the ground, crawling, knees digging into the coarse dirt.

She got to her feet and started to run. She wasn't sure what direction she was going. Didn't matter to her, so long as it was *away* from the beast.

Behind her, another howl tore through the woods. She felt it at her back, felt the gust of putrid, meat-stained breath on her neck.

Oh, God! It's right behind me!

Tammy tucked her chin, bent forward, and pumped her legs. Her bare feet slapped the earth. She ignored the jabbing bits of forest debris and pushed herself to move. She could no longer hear the deep breaths and rugged breathing behind her.

She stole a glance over her shoulder. In her bouncing vision, she saw the dark woods were clear. Streamers of fog were all that was there.

It's gone!

She wouldn't let the small victory slow her down. She'd seen enough movies. About the time she thought she'd made it to safety, the monster would attack. No, she had to keep moving. Couldn't stop until she was certain she was in the clear.

Tammy continued to run for a long time. Eventually, she reached a small clearing. She spotted a ruined tent, and a dwindled campfire that was mostly red glowing sticks. Confused, Tammy stopped running. Her lungs felt tight and cold as she panted.

Tammy walked into the clearing. On the ground was a dead body, its guts pulled out and the throat had been gouged into a fleshy gulley.

At first, she thought she'd found another site that had been attacked by the wolf. Then she realized the mangled remains was what was left of Russ.

I'm back at the campsite!

"Oh, shit…" Tammy grabbed a handful of her hair and held it. She'd run a complete circle. "Stupid, Tammy. So stupid!"

She looked around. She couldn't remember what direction she'd run off in the first time. She picked another route and prepared to run.

Then was slammed from the side.

She went down, sprawling. Her back pounded the ground. The large wolf came down on top of her, its gray fur smearing across her. Strands went into her mouth that tasted like mold. She felt the sticky firmness of its cock prodding her belly through her shirt.

Screaming, Tammy pounded her fists on its head. The wolf didn't seem to notice. She snatched back her arms to avoid its snapping snout. Teeth clacked together, spattering her with foamy drool. Claws ripped her shirt and bra in a brutal swipe, exposing her breasts. She saw a red puddle beginning to spread between the two mounds from a single, half inch rent in the slope of her left breast.

Its claws swiped her again, ripped a chunk of her shorts and sent it flailing away. She slapped and hit and kicked, bucked and thrashed as the wolf snapped its jaws, teeth clacking. It bit and clawed at everything she put in its way to protect herself: hands, arms, knees, and feet.

It forced its way between her thighs, spreading its legs to hold hers open. She could feel the tacky plumpness of its cock against her groin. The wolf reared back its head, howled, and was about to thrust.

CH-CHK!

The wolf paused, its wedge-shaped ears, discolored with gray hair, perked up. It turned. Saw something it didn't like and peeled back its narrow black lips and growled.

A loud blast shook the night. The wolf's head exploded in a mess of fur, pulpy clumps, and blood. Tammy's face was splashed in the chunky spray.

The werewolf was now headless, its neck a jagged stump spouting blood. Its thick arms still reached out, hands opening closing as if squeezing something invisible.

The body toppled forward, hitting the ground beside Tammy. Its neck continued to spurt across the dirt.

"You all right?" A man's voice.

Tammy blinked blood out of her eyes. The man stood over her, staring down. He wore an orange hunting cap, pulled down far enough to push out his ears. He looked to be in his sixties, with a light brush of gray stubble on his face. He held a shotgun, finger on the trigger. Smoke curled out from the barrel.

Tammy tried to speak, but couldn't stop crying.

"Ma'am?" The man cleared his throat. "Ma'am?"

"I'm...sorry..." She sniffled, wiped her eyes. Instead of drying the tears, she smeared more blood, turning her vision a splotchy red. "I don't mean to cry."

"It's okay. That fella over there in pieces belong to you?"

Tammy nodded, using what was left of her sleeve to wipe her face. "Boyfriend..."

"My condolences. That damn werewolf's been causing all sorts of havoc out here. Got a bunch of my cattle. Killed some hikers a month back. One of them was my granddaughter. Been coming out here with my dogs ever since. I've almost gotten it once or twice before. I'm all that's left. Bastard got my dogs."

Tammy sniffled. "So...it really was a..." Even after everything she'd endured, she still felt silly knowing what she was about to say. "A werewolf?"

"Matter of fact," said the man. "Yep."

72

"You saved me."

"Just doing my part."

Tammy felt more tears welling in her eyes. They spilled over, trickling down her cheeks. She was safe. Poor Russ didn't make it, but somehow, thanks to this man, she had. She would never forget Russ. She would make it her mission to ensure that no one forgot how wonderful he was.

"What's that?" asked the man.

Tammy noticed he was staring at her chest. She looked down and saw why. Nothing but shredded rags draped her crimson-slicked breasts. It looked as if she'd smeared herself in strawberry syrup. She tried to cover herself better, but there wasn't enough shirt left to do so. She noticed the slash on the side of her breast. Above that, between her collarbone and the top of her breast, a chunk of skin was missing. She saw circles denting the skin around the wound.

"I don't know," she said. "It doesn't really hurt."

She noticed the wound was starting to shrink.

"What the…?"

The man's eyebrows curled, the tips intersecting at the bridge of his nose. "You've been bit!"

"Have I?" she said. She didn't feel as if she'd been bitten. In fact, she felt pretty good. Probably better than she had all day. The soreness in her muscles was gone. She felt no pain from her injuries, either. The slash on her breast sealed before her eyes.

Strange.

She looked up at the man to ask him if he knew what was happening to her but her words choked in her throat when she saw she was gazing into the barrel of his shotgun.

"Sir…?"

"You've been bit."

"But…I…"

"You're going to change." He jacked a round into the chamber. "Never takes long. See? That one I just shot. That was my granddaughters' fiancé. He killed the one that attacked him and my granddaughter. But he was bit, too."

"For the love of God," she said. "I'm not going to change into a were…" She stopped talking when she lifted her hand and saw how it had begun to stretch. Peach-colored hair was sprouting from her wrist, spreading up her arm like moss. "Oh, no…"

She looked up at the man again.

He jacked a round into the chamber. "May God have mercy on your soul, lady."

Before Tammy could respond, the man pulled the trigger. The last thing Tammy saw was the flash. She never heard the shot.

Story Notes:

Another story that was originally written for an anthology with a monster-in-the-woods theme. This time, the anthology was canned before I could submit it. I later adapted the story into a script for a short film that I wanted to shoot, but that was also canned.

When I first began talks about this collection with the original publisher, I knew it would be one the stories I wanted to include. It's a bit silly, with an ending that might upset people, but it's a lot of fun and I had a blast writing it. In my mind, I was paying tribute to Gary Brandner, one of my favorite writers of all time.

THE WAGER

I'd been playing Xbox for about an hour when Claire came home. She walked into the living room of our one-bedroom apartment, her keys dangling from her fingers like bulky jewelry.

"Hey, Paul."

"Hey, babe," I said without tearing my eyes away from the TV.

"Is that the new wrestling game?"

"Yeah…" At least that's what I think I said, though I can't be sure. Couldn't take my eyes away from the screen. I was playing as The Mortician and had been battling Brain Damaged Dan inside a steel cage.

"Want to go against *me*?" she asked, tossing her keys on the coffee table. They slid to a stop in front of me, reminding me of westerns where the drifter enters a saloon and tosses a coin on the bar.

Pausing the game, I looked at her. I saw flashes each time I blinked from staring at the screen for so long. "But I'm in the middle of a match."

She puckered out her bottom lip. A trick that usually worked on me, because it meant if I caved, I'd probably get some reward sex for it. "Please?"

"All right."

"Yay!" Clapping her hands, she trotted to the couch and plopped down beside me. "Want me to join in this match, or start a new one?"

I decided to start a new one. With the game still paused, I scrolled down to *End Game* and selected it. I did a pretty good job of hiding my irritation at having to stop the match early.

Now before you start blaming me for being an asshole husband, let me point out that the reason I was dreading our match was simple—Claire was better than me at games. Didn't matter what game we played, she had a natural ability for kicking my ass. I could apply years of acquired strategy, and she'd simply defeat me by pressing buttons in no particular order, following it up with hours of pretentious sportsmanship afterward.

So imagine my shock when I actually won. And not just the first match, but five in a row! I was very humble about my success as I pointed at her and laughed in her face.

"Let's play again," she said.

That was when I should have had enough intelligence to call it a night, but I didn't. I was on a roll. "Aren't you tired of me making you look bad?"

Anger flashed across her face, intense and scary for a moment. Then it was gone. I wasn't too stupid to see she was getting upset with losing so much, but I *was* too stupid that I didn't stop when I was ahead.

"You're not making me look bad," she said. Strands of wavy red had fallen out of her ponytail, sprigs hanging by her eyes. Sweat had beaded above her lip, and her blue eyes were glossy with frustrated tears, but to me, she'd never looked more adorable. "I'm just getting warmed up. I think I'll kick your ass this time."

How could I back down from that challenge?

I stuck with the Mortician, and she chose Red Devil, The Mortician's revenge-obsessed brother. It was a good match, but she lost. Again. When the number three flashed on the screen, signaling the end of the match, I hopped up and strutted around the apartment like Ric Flair, even throwing out some of his prevalent *Whoos!*

Again, she challenged me, and again I beat her. We kept this up for a long time, only stopping long enough to heat up some microwavable dinners and guzzle a couple of sodas. We returned to the living room with a bag of chips and a two liter for us to share.

We played three more times.

"One more," she said as I stood up to shut off the game. "Just…one…more." Her shoulders rose and dropped with each heavy breath.

"No more after this," I said. "I'm starting to get a headache."

"Okay," she said.

I sat back down on the couch, ready to beat her one last time.

On the game, the bell rang. I made my character run at her. My fingers clicked the buttons, making the character's arm swing out. This time, Claire ducked it. I heard her fingers tap in a combo.

On screen I watched her character duck down, reach his arm through mine's legs, and catch him. Then he pulled back, rolling my character up. The ref dropped to his knees and began to pound the mat.

I hit the A and B buttons to kick out.

The ref slapped the mat a third time. I was stunned.

It was her turn to hop up and strut. Her large breasts bounced under her shirt, and when she leaned over her pants pulled tight against her rump.

I enjoyed the show, just not the motives behind it.

"Want to play again?" she asked.

Damn right I did!

She won again. What the hell was happening? I'd be damned if this would keep up.

We played again.

I lost again.

Her little victory dances became annoying.

She challenged me again, and I accepted. This time, I came up victorious, just barely. It had been by count out, so Claire argued that it didn't count. But at the end of the match, my hand was raised, so to me it counted just fine.

"Let's play again," she said.

"I'm tired of playing…"

"Tired of getting beat, you mean."

"I won that last one!"

"That hardly counts as a win. A *real* win is putting me down for a three count."

"Technically, I put you down for a *ten* count."

"Don't give me that shit. You hit me with a chair when the ref was down, then crawled back into the ring as he was waking up. That's bullshit."

"It happens all the time in real wrestling. Besides, I'm getting tired. It's almost midnight. I'm off the day after tomorrow, so we can play all night tomorrow night."

Claire gnawed at her bottom lip for a bit. Then she excitedly snapped her finger. "How about we have *one* more match."

"I just said…"

"Hear me out. *One* more match, and if I win, you have to do exactly what I want in the bedroom…"

I liked where this was going. "And if I win?"

"I have to do exactly what *you* want."

"Deal."

And fuck it all, I lost. I didn't really care she'd cheated to win, because I still felt like I was the real winner because I'd soon learn what secret fantasy she'd been harboring. At times, we could get aggressive and freaky in our sexual festivities, so I was looking forward to what she would say.

Claire turned to me, crawled up on the couch. I felt her warm breath tickling my ear as she said, "In ten minutes, meet me in the bedroom with your cat."

Before I could respond to her odd request, Claire hopped to her feet, twirled around to face me, and removed her shirt. She tossed it at my head, missing by an inch. Her busty chest was being smothered behind her bra, so she removed that as well. Her breasts fell out, full and springy. Her nipples were tiny hard points. "Ten minutes."

"Um…"

Claire hurried out of the room. I heard some clattering in the kitchen as cabinets opened and closed, then the quick trample of her feet as she headed to the bedroom. Then I couldn't hear anything at all.

As if knowing her company was required, Vivian Purrbox appeared and rubbed against my leg. I picked her up, then sat back, placing the fluffy cat on my lap. She immediately lay on her stomach, and I stroked her orange and white fur.

What was Claire planning? I tried conjuring up explanations. All of them were gross. Was *this* her fantasy? A bestiality threesome?

Maybe if I pretended it wasn't *my* cat...

I shook my head.

How could Vivian Purrbox and I look at each other the same?

Ten minutes finally passed. I carried my purring cat with me down the hall to the bedroom I shared with my wife. The door was closed, and I didn't want to just barge in if she wasn't ready, so I lightly knocked.

"Come in," Claire said from inside, her voice coy and mysterious.

I opened the door. The room was inundated in an orange glow from several candles that had been placed throughout the room. It felt ten degrees warmer in here than the rest of the apartment.

I looked around as I stepped inside.

"Shut the door so she doesn't run out," added Claire.

I obliged.

Naked, Clare lay on her side, on top of trash bags she'd spread across the bed. The improvised tarp made crinkling sounds as Claire stretched. Her skin looked milky in the candlelight. She was hairless from the shoulders down, with her crimson-colored locks hanging around her shoulders like spiral curtains.

She looked amazing.

"Wha-what do you want me to do?" I asked.

"Take off your clothes."

Stripping while holding a cat was not an easy task. But I managed to do so without dropping Vivian Purrbox or falling down.

When I was naked, Claire sat up. Crawling towards me, the plastic squeaked under her knees. "Don't drop the cat."

"Uh…"

She took me into her mouth and began to suck. Although I was extremely uncomfortable in the present situation, my soldier stood erect, proud and ready to serve.

With her mouth full, she spoke. "Likey?"

"God, yes…"

"Mmmm…" She sucked a moment longer, then pulled her mouth away with a wet popping sound. "Here."

She raised a knife up to me. I could see my sweaty, puzzled reflection in the blade.

"Take this and cut your cat open so she can bleed out on my skin."

My penis retracted like measuring tape. I pulled away from her and stumbled against the dresser behind me. Vivian Purrbox, oblivious to Claire's morbid request, purred softly in my arms. "What the hell did you just say?"

Claire got on her knees, resting a hand on her glossy thigh and pointing at me with the knife. "I won. So you have to do what I want in the bedroom."

"You *tricked* me."

"Don't be mad."

"You want me to pour my cat's blood all over you!"

"Don't be *mad*."

"How can I *not* be mad?"

"I'm not a freak."

"This is pretty damn freaky, if you ask me."

"That damn cat hates me. She's tried to kill me."

This wasn't the first time Claire had claimed Ms. Purrbox was an attempted murderer. At least twice a week Claire would make such far-fetched accusations.

"How many times does she get right in front of me when my hands are full?"

"Cats just do that."

"She's trying to trip me, hoping I'll break my neck. And what about that time I was listening to music in the bathtub? She tried to knock the radio in the water!"

"Claire."

"I know you'd never get rid of her unless…"

"So this was just a ruse to get me to kill my cat? You planned this all along, didn't you?"

"Not at first, but…" She nibbled on her bottom lip.

"But what?"

"Well, I knew you were going to pick up the game today, so while I was at work I looked up some gamer channels and watched them play so I would know what to do."

"Claire, you didn't."

"I did. I let you win all those matches."

I should've known. I'd never been able to beat her before, so why had I thought I'd suddenly acquired the talent to do so. "Damn it, Claire."

"I feel awful."

"You really should. Because it *is* awful."

Claire's head dipped. Every so often she glanced up at me with her lovely eyes. As angry as I was, I sort of understood why she'd taken this route. She really hated Vivian Purrbox, and I was pretty sure the cat's feelings were mutual. But I also knew Claire wouldn't really make me go through with it. What she was asking was inhumane. And she really wasn't an evil person.

"Here," Claire said, reaching for me. "I'll suck on you to help keep your mind off of it."

Evil bitch!

She grabbed at my shriveled sniper, but I pulled away again. "This isn't going to happen," I told her.

"You have to keep your end of the bet."

"Not really. You just admitted to cheating."

"I did not cheat! I won and you have to do what I want."

"But why like this? Why her blood all over you?"

"That way I can bathe in her death...I want to smear her patronizing essence all over me, absorb the finality in knowing I've beaten her."

What kind of dark-magic bullshit she was talking about?

"And I'll have you all to myself," she added.

So that was it? She was jealous of a damn cat. Vivian had come to live with me long before I'd even met Claire. So she knew what she was getting when she agreed to spend her life with me.

But Claire was the one I'd married. Someday she'd be the mother of my children. We'd grow old together. Vivian was already old. She maybe had a few years left on her. Tops. This could be considered a mercy killing to prevent the cat from suffering later.

I lowered the blade to Vivian Purrbox. A quick glance at Claire, and I saw she was smiling. I looked back down at Ms. Purrbox. She lifted her head, eyes squinting. She sniffed the knife's shiny surface, then turned away, already bored with it.

"Paul. Don't stall this any longer. I want the cat's dead blood on me!"

My wife was absolutely bananas. "Let's play one more match." Claire showed me her teeth. "*One* more match, and if I win, we forget this ever happened."

"And if I win?" she asked.

"I'm not killing the cat I've had for almost ten years so you can bathe in her blood!"

"Fine!" Claire sat back on the bed, folding her arms over her chest. The pouting stance squished her breasts. "If I win, I get to cut off your pinky toe."

"Are you completely insane?"

"It's your toe or your goddamn cat. Your choice."

"I choose neither."

"Then I'm going to go stay with my mother."

Jesus, not her. If Claire went to her mom's, I'd never see her again. Didn't matter if I told my mother-in-law the ultimatum Claire had given me. She'd side with her daughter.

Well, you should've slit that old cat wide open for Claire and doused my sweet daughter in its essence!

"Fine. Pinky toe it is."

Claire looked disappointed. "Really? You'd rather cut off your damn pinky toe?"

"I don't want you to leave, so if that's what it takes to keep you here…"

"Just kill the fucking cat."

"Can't I just get rid of her?"

"No. I have to know she's dead. She'll come back and you'd let her stay."

"No, she wouldn't."

"Paul, I've taken her away many times and she always comes back."

"You…what?" First I'd heard about that. "You've tried to ditch my cat behind my back?"

"She tries to smother me when I sleep!"

"Claire, I think when this is over, you're going to have to see a shrink or something."

"I'm not crazy." Even as she said it, I noticed a nutty twitch in her eye. This worried me more than I wanted to accept.

"The cat is not being butchered. We'll play the damn game your way."

"Remember, you asked for this."

"I did not. *You* did."

"Whatever."

Claire walked around the room, huffing out all the candles.

Neither one of us bothered to get dressed. Naked, we sat next to each other on the couch, tongues poking through our lips in serious concentration. The only sounds were our thumbs clacking across the buttons of the controllers and the intense cheers of the audience in the game.

After a mostly one-sided battle, Claire had me in the kitchen, a cutting board under my foot and a meat cleaver in her hand. The way she lopped off my pinky toe without hardly a flinch was disconcerting, but that feeling was quickly outweighed by the hot pain blasting up my foot.

Blood sprayed Claire's breasts as she knelt between my legs, watching me scream and hop around the kitchen like a parent that had just spanked her kid for the first time. I slipped in my blood and landed on my side hard enough to shake the fridge. If I would have been watching this on TV, I would've found it comical, even somewhat erotic, but thanks to the pain of losing a toe, eroticism and humor was the farthest thing from my mind.

After my agonizing tantrum through the kitchen, I felt dizzy. Claire bandaged my foot without speaking. When she applied the last bit of tape to hold the gauze on, she clucked her tongue. "Should've killed the cat. Now you have to come up with a story about how you lost your toe when I take you to the hospital."

Claire took a small container from the cupboard, then filled it with ice. She plucked my toe from the cutting board and dropped it on the ice.

"Rematch," I said.

"Paul, it's over. You need a doctor so he can reattach it. It's a clear cut, so there shouldn't be any problems." She snapped her fingers. "That's it! You were chopping veggies and dropped the cleaver on your foot. That'll work."

"After the rematch," I said.

"Are you that obsessed with winning that you'd risk another wager?"

I stared at her, unable to remind her it was her obsession that put me in this predicament in the first place. After a few minutes of back and forth, we'd settled on a new wager: her pinky toe against either my left foot or my cat's head. I accepted the bet on my foot. No way was I going to kill my cat, and no way was I going to cut off my foot. This had to stop somewhere.

We played the game, and I won. I could tell Claire hadn't allowed it to happen this time from the way she gripped the controller, causing the plastic casing to pop.

I chopped off her toe in an even more emotionless manner than she had mine. The gratification I felt watching her writhe around the floor, slipping in her blood, was intoxicating. I felt as if I was on ecstasy—or what I imagined the drug to feel like since I'd never taken it—and every pore in my body was alive and tingling.

I had sex with her right on the floor in her blood. At first, she didn't like it, but I bet her she'd have an orgasm before me. The wager? Either she apologized to Vivian Purrbox, or we had to play the damn game again, and make a new wager.

Less than five minutes, I was spurting inside her.

I lost the bet.

Afterwards, we cleaned up the kitchen, then I bandaged up her foot and dropped her toe in the container with mine. We took some aspirin for the pain, then returned to the living room. Vivian Purrbox was sleeping soundly on the arm of the couch. I sat next to her, and Claire on the other side of me.

"What do you want to bet?" I asked.

"I'm really mad at you."

"At me?"

Claire nodded, mouth twisted to the side and her lips pursed. "Very."

"What the hell I'd do?"

"Well…you cut of my toe. And the rape on the kitchen floor."

"You cut off mine first! And that was hardly rape. Quit being so dramatic."

"Fine. It wasn't rape, but you still cut off my toe."

"Again, you cut off mine *first*."

"Because you wouldn't…"

"Yeah, yeah. Kill my cat. I know."

Claire punched the couch cushion. "Just kill her and we can stop this!"

Flinching, I looked around as if people were standing all around us. "A little louder. I don't think the tenants on the bottom floor heard you!"

"Okay. You want a wager? Fine. If I win, I get to cut off your damn cock."

I stared at her. No way was she serious. But the look on her face, the coldness, the hollow stare in her eyes, told me she was very serious. "Claire. Listen to yourself."

"I heard what I said just fine. Either your proud member, which I might add is quite magnificent, or the cat. If you don't want to cut off her head, just drown her in the toilet or something."

"I can't believe how cruel you are."

"I'm not cruel! You are because you don't love your wife."

"So because I won't slaughter an old, half-deaf cat for you, I don't love you?"

"People do stuff they hate for their spouses all the time. Not you, apparently."

"And if I don't agree to this, my only other option is letting you take the meat cleaver to my privates?"

"Right."

"What if I win?"

Claire shrugged. "It's not going to happen."

"Sound pretty sure of yourself."

"I am."

I nodded. "Okay. Fine. If I win, you have to kiss Vivian Purrbox on the nose and tell her how sorry you are. Then you have to let her sleep in the bed with us every night until she finally passes away by natural causes."

"No."

"Then no bets." I sat back, crossing my arms. "It's up to you."

Claire turned away from me. I could hear a soft growl forming in her throat. After a few minutes, she stood up and walked to the TV. She grabbed the controllers and turned on the Xbox.

We selected our usual characters. In the menu, we turned off the time limit, made it a No DQ match, and set the stipulations to pinfall and submission only.

After fifteen minutes of back-and-forth brutality, I pinned Claire in the middle of the ring.

Instead of gloating, I set the controller down and turned to her. "I don't ever want to play this game again. Okay?"

Claire stared at the TV, her mouth twitching.

"Listen," I said, "the wager is off. I'm not going to make you kiss the cat. She doesn't have to sleep with us. But this competition is done. I'm willing to move past it, if you are. To be honest, it's going to take a long time for me to forget about it. But, in the meantime, we have to think of a story to tell the ER staff about our toes. The cutting veggies story isn't going to work now since your toe is missing, too."

Claire dropped the controller. Stood up. "A bet's a bet." She rolled her head on her shoulders, cracking her neck. Flexing her hands, she moved her arms as if she were warming up for a fight.

"No," I said. "It's not. It's over. Let's get dressed and drive to the ER. We can figure it all out on the way."

"First thing's first," she said, turning around to face Vivian. She looked down at the sleeping cat. "Just a kiss on the nose, right?"

I sighed. "Right."

"Then it's over. I'll shake your hand and be done with it."

"We won't be done with it for a long time," I said. I was afraid of what kind of repercussions this night would have on our future. But I was also too tired and in too much pain to worry about it.

Claire took a deep breath and let it slowly out through nose. "Here I go." She sunk to a crouch in front of Vivian's face. "You love him and so do I, right?"

Vivian's eyes cracked open. She yawned.

"How about a truce?" said Claire.

Vivian Purrbox titled her head. I noticed a soft purr emanating from her fluffy midsection. I smiled at the sight of my two favorite women finally deciding to put an end to their feud.

My smile tilted when Vivian suddenly launched from the couch with a high-pitched yowl, all four legs spread wide, her tail erect and fluffed out. Claire barely had the chance to open her mouth to attempt a scream before the cat latched onto her face.

"Vivian!" I yelled.

But I was too late. Claire was already on her feet and spinning, pulling at the cat with both hands. Her front claws were sunk into either side of Claire's scalp while the bottoms were digging into her neck.

I ran over to the twirling twosome, reaching out, but Claire's shoulder whammed my chest. Staggering my back, my feet tangled together, and I fell backwards. My back hit the coffee table, busting through the glass before pounding the floor.

The impact hadn't only sent me down, it had caused Claire to stumble to the side. Her shoulder hit the window first. The glass shattered. The blinds folded outward. Claire's knees hit the sill, knocking her feet out.

The last thing I saw was Claire and Vivian toppling through the window and vanishing on the other side. We were four stories up, so the dull splat of their landing on the concrete walkway below was faint.

I wanted to get up and go downstairs, but I couldn't move. I noticed a jagged blade of glass, slicked in my blood, was jutting from my stomach. I wasn't going anywhere. From the heavy amount of blood spouting from the wound, I knew I'd probably be dead before anybody came to check on me.

Shaking my head, I realized I should have just done what Claire had wanted all along.

I should've killed the cat.

Story Notes:

A long time ago, I read a tabloid article about a man's wife who was dangerously jealous of his cat and attacked him because he wouldn't get rid of it. I never forgot that and wasn't surprised when it popped up while writing the story.

BLACK GARBAGE BAGS

Mama hollered for me at lunchtime. It was summer vacation in 1993, and I'd been outside most of the morning, doing chores in the awful heat. I headed inside, washed my hands, and sat at the table. My parents had already eaten, so there was only one plate with a ham and cheese sandwich and potato chips on the side.

It took no time for me to clean my plate.

As I chugged a can of Pepsi, Lee, our German Shepard started barking. He wasn't one of those dogs that barked at every little scuttle or scamper. Since we lived on a private dirt road in the woods, his barking most likely meant we had a visitor.

Behind me, Mama was washing the dishes. She paused, hands in the water, and tilted her head. "Somebody here?" she asked.

"Don't know," I said.

I stood up and walked into the living room where a large bay window looked out on our front yard and the hay field beyond it. I spotted a car, the sunlight glinting off the windshield. It was white and brown with a bar on top.

The driver's side door swung open. Sheriff Wilson clambered out with some difficulty because of his fleshy size. He adjusted his wide hat. He wore reflective sunglasses and a tan shirt with dark brown pants. He slid his nightstick through the clip on the side of his belt. His handgun on the other side gleamed under the intense July sun.

"Who's out there, Doug?" My father's voice. Though he'd spoken in a normal tone, I flinched as if he'd shouted.

I looked at him from over my shoulder. He stood in the doorway, frowning.

"It's Sheriff Wilson," I told him. "He's in the front yard."

I saw something flicker in his eyes just for a moment, then it was gone. "Stay inside," he said. He walked to the front door. I looked back and forth from him to the window as Sheriff Wilson sauntered through the yard. Lee, familiar with our visitor, pranced around him as he walked, sniffing his calves and shoes with each step.

"Why do you think he's here, Daddy?"

"Remember what I said. Stay inside."

He pulled open the door, booted the screen door open, and went outside. The screen door whacked the house when it closed.

Mama stepped into the living room. She was absently wiping her already dry hands with a towel. She looked as if she were unaware of anything going on around her.

"I'm going to my room," I said.

If she'd heard me, she gave no indication.

In my room, I shut and locked the door. I had to find out what the sheriff wanted to see Daddy about. This wasn't the first time Sheriff Wilson had come to visit. He'd been to a few of my birthday parties, and since my thirteenth was coming up in a little over a week, I assumed he would be by then as well. But this visit felt different. I sensed it the moment I saw the car.

I went over to my window, slid the curtains over, and unlocked it. The air conditioning was on, so my window had been closed for nearly a month now. I tried raising it quietly, but it made a loud popping sound as it flung high. I bit down on my bottom lip, waiting for Mama to come asking what I was up to.

She never came.

I waited another minute to be sure, then I gripped the latches on the screen between my thumb and index finger and lifted it enough for me to squeeze through.

My feet slapped the ground. I stood there, waiting. My room was at the side of the house. If I went to the left, I'd end up in the front yard where Daddy and Sheriff Wilson were. I could hear them talking, but couldn't understand what they were saying.

I *needed* to know what they were talking about.

Hunched over, I snuck my way to the corner of the house. I could see them. Dad stood with his arms crossed, nodding while Sheriff Wilson talked.

"How's the Chevelle coming along?" asked Sheriff Wilson.

"Why don't you come see it," said Daddy, laughing.

Then they turned toward me and started walking.

I almost shouted. My heart pounded. I scurried away from the house, spinning circles as I looked around. There was nowhere I could go. It would take too long to climb back into my room. There was a field beside the house. No way could I make it over there without them seeing me.

Their voices were getting louder. They were so close now.

I ran for Daddy's shop. It was behind the house, next to our garden. I hadn't put up the lawnmower yet from when I was doing chores, so the garage door was still open.

Inside, I looked around for a place to hide. I could see Daddy and the sheriff heading toward the shop through the small window that faced the house. The only place was inside the Chevelle that was parked a few feet from me, but I didn't want to go hide in there because that was where they were heading.

But it was my only option.

I quietly opened the door, and slid into the backseat. I reached over, pulled the door shut. It was stifling inside the car, hard to breathe from the closed windows. I had been sweating before, but now it was pouring down my body.

I squeezed myself into the floorboard. Being tall for my age, I had to bend my knees to get on my side, then I slid back against the passenger door. It was awkward and uncomfortable, but I was certain I'd be out of sight.

I'd just gotten settled when they entered. Since I was tucked so far down, I couldn't see them.

"Then I put the tires back on," Daddy said. "Probably after church tomorrow, I'll take her for a spin. Drive her into town to get the paper."

"Sounds fine," Sheriff Wilson said. "Although, you could save yourself some trouble if you'd just subscribe to the paper. You know, they drop it right off in your front yard."

Their voices became louder as they neared the car. Sheriff Wilson popped into my view at the window. He turned around to face my father, putting his back to me.

"Well," Daddy said, "out here, they're only willing to drop it off at the end of the dirt road. We tried it before, and that damn Ellison kept tossing ours into the ditch."

Ellison was one of our few neighbors. He lived at the very end of the dirt road with his mother. Over forty and very overweight, I recognized his laziness even as a kid.

"Well, if you knocked him on his ass, I'd look the other way." Sheriff Wilson laughed. I could hear Daddy laughing as well. "That son of a bitch would have sure deserved it."

"Wish I would have known that then."

They shared another laugh. It died in the air, leaving an uncomfortable silence that I could feel even inside the car.

Sheriff Wilson groaned. "I guess we should stop with this pretend chit-chat and get down to business, huh?"

"Yeah, I suppose so."

The mood became as thick as the heat.

Sheriff Wilson cleared his throat before he began. "I know you're familiar with Pete and Ellie Robinson. The family that lives on the other side of the woods?"

"Sure, I am. I bump into Pete at the parts store a lot. They have a little girl…"

"Yes. Allison. Nine. She's been missing for two days now."

Daddy was quiet. I felt a sickening flutter in my stomach.

Sheriff Wilson nodded. "Ellie let her play in the backyard for a little bit. When she went to call her in, she was gone. It was as if she'd vanished into thin air."

"Why hasn't it been in the paper?"

"We're keeping it hush-hush."

"That doesn't make any sense, John. It seems you'd want this getting out."

"Not just yet. Hell, everyone in town knows who Allison is. If they were to see her walking around, they'd just call the parents."

"But you don't think anyone will see her walking around. Do you?"

"No. I don't, I'm afraid to say."

"Then why are you telling *me* all of this?"

The Sheriff sighed. I could tell he was dreading saying what had to be said next. "I think you know why I'm telling you all of this."

Daddy said nothing.

The Sheriff continued. "We haven't allowed it to go to print just yet, because we wanted to be sure of something first."

"Of what?" Daddy's tone had hardened.

"The facts."

Daddy was quiet a moment. Then he said, "If you have something to say, then say it."

"I don't want to say it. That's the problem." Removing his hat, he rubbed his hand through his gray, sweat-drenched hair. Then he put the hat back on. "Her parents were a mess last night. We set out with a search party and combed the woods. When we went to meet up this morning at the starting point, they didn't show. The parents, I mean. So we went looking again and found their bodies near Cripple Creek. Hacked up with an axe."

My skin went prickly.

An axe.

"It was a messy attack. Very violent. But the axe wounds were clean, as if the blade was brand new. And I remembered running into you at Anderson's Hardware last month. You were buying a new axe. I think I remember you said the old one wouldn't hardly cut paper anymore."

"It had gotten dull."

"Where's the axe? I'm going to need to see it."

"Are you sure?"

"I'm afraid so. I could come back with a warrant, but I don't want to do that. Nobody knows I'm here. Figured it'd be best if I came to check things out first, since we've known each other for so long. No sense in dragging anybody else into this if we don't have to."

I heard Daddy sigh. Then he said, "You're more than welcome to see the axe. It's over there, beside the weed-eater. The blade's just been cleaned."

"Has it, now?"

"This morning, to be precise."

"I see."

Sheriff Wilson turned his back to Daddy. I saw him from the side now, his gut drooping over his belt. He'd only taken one step toward the axe when Daddy lunged for him. He wrapped his arm around the sheriff's throat, sliding the other under the sheriff's arm to block him from going for his gun.

For an older man, he seemed to be strong. He shook from side to side, twisted his hips. He attempted to flip Daddy over his shoulder, but couldn't get in the position right. He stumbled forward and banged against the Chevelle. His face hit the window, smooshing flat against the glass.

The sheriff saw me. His eyebrows curled over his wide eyes. Over his shoulder, I could see Daddy applying pressure to the Sheriff's neck. Gagging, Sheriff Wilson's eyes bulged. Daddy's face flushed while Sheriff Wilson's turned blue as it smeared across the glass, wiping his spit all over.

The Sheriff's eyes rolled back in his head, showing only the milky whites. Daddy squeezed him a little longer. Then he let the poor man drop. Hands on his hips, he stood outside the Chevelle, panting.

Then he jerked the door open and leaned inside the car. "I told you to stay *inside*."

"I'm suh-sorry, Daddy."

"You've got a lot to be sorry about. Get out of there."

Nodding, I scrambled out of the car. I moved to the side, away from Daddy. He looked mad enough to take the belt to my ass. He threw the door shut hard enough to shake the car.

I glanced down at the sheriff's body. His face was the color of a plum.

"I didn't want to have to do that," said Daddy. "He left me no choice…"

"I…know, Daddy. I'm sorry."

Daddy spun around to me so quickly that I thought he was about to come after me. He pointed a finger, and I flinched as if it were a gun. "Get your butt inside and send your Mama out here. We'll deal with you later."

"Okay…"

I ran inside with tears welling in my eyes and told Mama what Daddy said. She was drinking a beer and stared at me over the can upturned to her mouth. Putting down the beer, she didn't take her eyes off me. I could tell she was ashamed, and that destroyed me knowing what she was thinking. As she headed for the back door, I went to my room and sat down on the bed. My window was still open, the screen pushed up. I realized Daddy had probably noticed it when he was leading the sheriff to his demise.

It was all my fault.

I never should've been in the woods the other day. I never should've walked to the Robinson's and hid behind a tree, watching, hoping I would get a glimpse of Mrs. Robinson in a bathing suit. It had happened before. Sometimes, when her husband wasn't home, she'd sunbathe naked, her body glistening under a sheen of oil. Her nipples would be hard points aimed at the sky.

Some nights, after my parents were asleep, I'd sneak over there and look through the windows. I'd watched the Robinsons having sex one of those nights, doing things on their bed I'd only seen on late-night TV. Mrs. Robinson's body, slick with sweat, her eyes screwed shut and her lips bowed as she moaned while her husband rammed into her from behind.

I knew I wouldn't be able to go peek in the windows, but I'd hoped just to catch a glimpse of Mrs. Robinson. Hoped she would be naked.

She wasn't out there, though.

Allison was. She spotted me behind the tree. Instead of running to tell her mother, she'd walked over to where I was hiding to ask what I was doing.

And she looked so much like her mother.

I shouldn't have lied about there being baby bunnies in the woods. She never would have followed me if she didn't think she was going to see their little fluffy bodies hopping around. And I wouldn't have been tempted to touch her. If I'd kept my hands to myself, she wouldn't have started screaming. I wouldn't have held her down and did *things* to her.

When I was finished, I was so scared she'd tell on me, I *had* to clobber her head with the rock. Just like Daddy *had* to kill Sheriff Wilson. She'd left me no other choice.

But I felt awful. Her blood was all over me. I came home and told Daddy what I'd done. I was surprised when he didn't call the sheriff. Sure, he was upset with me, and I knew I would be punished, but instead of handling it right then, he'd gone out to the woods himself.

I gave him a few minutes before I followed him to the spot where I'd left Allison. He began hacking her body to pieces with his new axe. He was putting the pieces into garbage bags when Mr. and Mrs. Robinson stumbled up on him and caught him in the middle of cleaning up their daughter's grisly remains.

And just like Allison, Mrs. Robinson started screaming.

Then Daddy used the axe on them and put their dismembered pieces in bags as well. But he ran out of bags to put their body parts in. I hurried back home. He returned several minutes later. I eavesdropped on him telling Mama what had happened. He'd told her she needed to get more trash bags in the morning. He said he'd hidden the bodies, and they should be fine until he could go back out there and finish up.

I guess he was unaware of the search party.

Sitting on my bed, I heard the back door open, followed by footsteps moving around in the kitchen. A couple minutes later, the door banged again. Unable to handle the waiting any longer, I went into the kitchen and looked out the window. I could see the shop at the edge of the yard. Mama was turning around as she stepped into the shop through the open garage side. Reaching up, she pulled down the garage door.

In one of her hands was a brand-new box of garbage bags.

Story Notes:
This was the first short story I completed after reading Bentley Little's *The Collection.* I'd attempted another one before it, but quickly realized

it was pure crap. I was gearing up to start working on the original draft of *The Lurkers*, but wanted to write something short before committing to another attempt at a novel. I wrote it in a day and was pretty pleased with it.

Shortly after that, my father passed away. Though he never killed a sheriff (that I know of), nor had to cover up anything evil that I'd done, the dad in this story was based on my own father. I've put my dad in other stories here and there, but this was the first and probably my favorite.

For a long time, the story was lost. A lot of emotional stress followed my dad's death. Plus, we moved into a new house the following year. When I finally decided I was strong enough to revisit it, I couldn't find it. Years later, and after another move to another house, I found the printed pages in a box and read over it. I was happy to find that I still liked the story. It needed a lot of tightening, but the foundation was solid. I put the pages away with plans to work on it after settling in.

I have yet to find those pages again. Thankfully, while searching a flash drive for something else almost a year ago, I came across the original file. What's in this collection is the polished version. I hope you enjoyed it.

BRUCE SMILEY'S ULTIMATE DEATH MACHINE

"That's a death machine?" Brandy asked.

The salesman smiled. The name tag pinned to his suit jacket told her his name was Marvin. "An *ultimate* death machine."

"Oh, right. You said that."

Marvin adjusted his tie. "All you do, is put in the name of someone you want to die by using the dial like this." He demonstrated by using his thumb to roll the dial until the name *John Doe* could be read inside the bar. The machine itself wasn't so much a machine as it was a device, a bulky handheld gadget that reminded Brandy of the calculator that held the paper roll on top. Her parents had one and only used it during tax season.

Nodding, Brandy feigned interest. She regretted opening the front door. She'd thought it was the UPS man delivering her vitamins. Every third Wednesday, he showed up around lunchtime with a small box. To her surprise, and now her annoyance, the UPS man was late. She'd tried to explain to the salesman she had no time for a demonstration, but he'd been pushy and was already halfway in the house before she could try closing the door on him.

She'd figured a few minutes wouldn't hurt.

Now she wanted him to leave. First chance she got, she was going to tell Marvin, the Salesman it was time for him to go.

"And then, you just remove this cap," he said, peeling back a plastic, pencil eraser-sized cap to reveal a sharp point. He pointed at it. "You have to prick your finger on this needle to give the machine a *little* blood. That's what makes it work." He set the machine on the coffee table that separated them. "You do that, then you wait. Simple."

Staring at the needle that was the girth of a coffee stirrer, she said, "It needs blood to work?"

"Yes. I mean, just consider it a quick, mostly painless blood offering to see your enemies fall."

Brandy frowned. She wondered if she should call the police. "I appreciate the demo, but I'm going to have to ask you to leave…"

"Surely there's *somebody* you want to face an ultimate death. Right?"

What kind of person did this guy think she was? She wasn't evil. She didn't start every day constructing a list of people she wouldn't mind being taken off the earth.

"I'm good," she said, "but thanks."

"Of course," said Marvin. He tugged at his green tie, then adjusted his thick black glasses. His dark gray suit and matching hat made Brandy think of the *Batman* villain, the Riddler.

"Well," said Marvin, clucking his tongue. "If you're sure there's nobody, then I can't let you *sample* the machine."

Brandy's eyebrows lifted. "Sample?"

"Right. At Bruce Smiley Industries, we care about the customer. And we would not even dream of selling something as profound as the Ultimate Death Machine if the customer couldn't try it out first."

"A freebie?"

"Correct."

Brandy laughed. "You're serious, aren't you?"

"Do I look like I'm joking?" Though he grinned, there was nothing on his face that suggested humor. His skin looked as if it didn't quite match his head, as if it were either the wrong size or belonged to someone else.

Why would I think that?

Brandy didn't know, but Marvin from Bruce Smiley Industries didn't seem real.

Maybe I'm dreaming.

She could only hope.

"I thank you for the offer, and the free sample, but I just couldn't even begin to think of somebody I'd want to…um…"

"Suffer an ultimate death?"

"Right."

"Too bad. Because somebody wanted *you* to suffer one."

A cold flutter worked through Brandy's chest. "What did you say?"

"Oh, sure. Just yesterday morning, to be precise."

"Who?"

Marvin wagged a finger. "What kind of salesman would I be to betray our honor code. That would be divulging private information, and I just couldn't..."

"I'll sample the machine if you tell me."

"Wanda Baker."

"That bitch."

Marvin smiled. "She didn't even have to think about it. When I'd convinced her the machine could work for her and offered her the free sample, your name just fired right out of her."

Heat flowed under Brandy's skin. She wouldn't have been surprised to see her flesh bubbling. "Let me guess. Because I got to go to Paris instead of her?"

"I'm sorry?"

"That's why she picked me. Right? We work together. Used to be pretty close, but we were both up for the trip to Paris for the training seminar and promotion. The higher-ups liked me better and picked me. I got the trip, the pay raise, and the nice office on the upper floor."

"Oh, that. It was your affair with Mr. Buxton and how you used the cell phone video of your sex acts to bribe your way into it that really upset her. She feels betrayed. But *she* doesn't understand competition in the workplace. It's a dog-eat-dog world, and you're a wolf."

Brandy's mouth dropped open. How the hell did Wanda even know about that? She hadn't told anyone other than Hal Buxton, that the video existed.

There's no way she could've known!

"So what, she thinks she's going to take my place with me out of the way?"

Marvin shrugged. "I just sell the machine, ma'am. I can't vouch for the customers' intentions. I like you, though, Brandy. Can I call you Brandy?" Before she could grant him permission, he was already talking again. "That's why I wanted to make sure you knew all you needed to know."

He removed his hat. His black hair was slicked back and shined in the light of the room. It looked as if he'd placed a helmet of glossy, dark plastic on his head.

"So, if you're sure you aren't interested in trying out the machine, then I will wish you a good day and be on my way."

He set the leather satchel he'd carried the machine inside of on the table, opened it, and lifted the machine. He was starting to put it in when Brandy stood up.

"Wait!"

The man looked up at her. A corner of his mouth lifted. "Yes?"

Brandy held out her finger. "I pick Wanda Baker."

"Good choice, Brandy." Marvin pushed the leather case aside. He pulled the Ultimate Death Machine to the center of the table, turned it around so the bulky gadget faced Brandy. It was tan in color, the dial on the side was like a small joystick, and the thumbtack-sized pricker was in the center of the bottom.

"I told you the name," she said.

"Yes, you did." He put on a sympathetic face. "But *you* have to be the one to put it into the machine."

"Oh."

"Yeah."

"Fine."

Brandy got on her knees in front of the coffee table. She tugged up her pants up to make sure her ass wasn't poking out the top. Then she put her hands on the device. The body felt cold as ice, and hard. Though it looked like the kind of thin material a DVD player would be made from, it felt as if it were bulletproof.

"So I just use this?" she asked, pinching the tips of the dial.

"Right. Up until you find the right letter, then click it to the right for the next. When you're done, you just push the dial in, like ringing a doorbell."

"Okay."

Moments ago, Brandy had been more than willing to see Wanda's name inside the narrow bar, but now that she knew she had to be the one to type it in, she wasn't so eager.

It's like pulling the trigger myself.

Then she realized that Wanda must not have been so hesitant with Marvin yesterday. She needed to beat Wanda or it meant her own ultimate death.

Brandy pushed the joystick up. Letters whirred by. She stopped on W.

"One down," said Marvin.

Brandy wiped the sweat from her brow. Then she gripped the stick again and found the next letter. She kept going until WANDA BAKER had been spelled out.

"The tiny blood offering," said Marvin.

Brandy gulped. She lowered her index finger down to the sharp point. It looked clean. The metal gleamed. She'd had her finger pricked more than once. It had always been a sharp sting, but quick. She doubted this would be much different.

She was wrong. It felt less like a sting and more like a bite. The pain shot up her arm, making it go instantly numb. But it was quickly forgotten when the dial started to spin. The ribbon inside had been white, but Brandy watched in shock as her blood striped it in red, giving it a candy cane appearance until it was completely crimson.

The dials stopped spinning. The red began to soak into the white until it could no longer be seen. She heard something like raspy laughter inside her head. It faded away as soon as it had begun.

When she looked at the dial again, it was white.

"Pleasure doing business with you," said Marvin.

"So that's it?" asked Brandy. She looked up. Marvin was setting the satchel back on the table. He reached into the flap inside the lid and brandished an odd knife that looked like bone with a wavy blade.

"Yes," he said. "The ultimate death has been ordered." He stood up, stepped around the table. "And now I have another customer's order that I must see fulfilled."

"Wanda's?" asked Brandy.

Marvin smiled. "Correct!" He held the knife up, smiling as he showed her the blade.

"But...I just told you I wanted her to...suffer..." Brandy was starting to feel strange. Her arm had gone numb and the tingling effect was working its way through her body.

"An ultimate death, right. But you seem to have forgotten, she ordered an ultimate death on you first.

Just because you ordered one on her doesn't *cancel* her order."

Brandy couldn't believe she hadn't realized that before. All of this had done nothing to deter her own fate.

"And now," said Marvin, "thanks to you, I can collect two deaths' commission. It's been a good month, and you have made it my best one yet! I figured that since Wanda had been so easy to coerce by telling her about your cell phone video, you would be just as quick to get back at her when you found out about her ultimate death request."

Confused, Brandy said, "You told her?" Marvin nodded. "How...did you know?"

"A good salesman thoroughly researches all his possible clients, Brandy. That's what makes me so good at my job."

Marvin crouched beside Brandy. He reached out and ripped her shirt open. Her breasts were covered by a bra which he used the knife to cut between the cups. The bra sagged, exposing her mounds to him.

Brandy wanted to cover herself, but couldn't move her arms. She could only sit there on her knees, watching as Marvin lowered the tip of the blade to her breasts.

"See, we're not selling the machine itself," he said. "That's sort of a common misunderstanding. We're selling the ultimate deaths themselves. The machine just sees to it that the deaths are carried out. Once you offer the blood, it's a done deal and, I'm afraid to say, there are no cancelations."

Brandy wanted to run away, but couldn't. She felt as if she'd been strapped to the floor.

"So I have one more question for you before you receive your ultimate death from Bruce Smiley Industries."

Brandy's throat felt swollen and dry. She couldn't find her voice.

"What kind of ultimate death would you like Wanda Baker to endure?" Marvin stared at her. A smile formed, curling the corners of his mouth. "Oh, you're a twisted girl."

Brandy wanted to tell him she hadn't said anything. But an image had flashed in Brandy's head of that knife being used on Wanda in areas that were meant for pleasure. Somehow, he'd known what she was thinking, just as he'd known about her cell phone videos.

Marvin laughed. It sounded much like the inhuman chortle she'd heard in her head moments ago. "I'm surprised you and Wanda didn't get along better. You're a lot alike. You want this knife to bring her to a bloody release. And she wanted your breasts cut off and shoved down your throat."

Brandy tried to scream. Couldn't. Her throat felt as if it were being slowly squeezed.

"And don't you worry none, Brandy. Soon as I'm done here, I'm going to head right over to Wanda Baker's house and deliver her ultimate death."

Smiling, Marvin lowered the blade to her right breast.

He began to slice.

Story Notes:
A silly little story that popped in my head one night while taking a shower. I've always wanted to write

one of those strange salesman-type stories and I thought this idea would work. I wrote it in one sitting, wearing the Bentley Little influence on my sleeve.

BEDSIDE MANNER

*M*elanie pulled at the duct tape strapping her arms to the bedposts. Might as well have been cement holding her there. "Please," she said through the gag. "Let me go!"

The man, bracing himself up by one arm between her legs, stroked her shin. The light from the ceiling left a shiny bar across his freshly shaved scalp. His chest-length beard was the color of pumpkins, and his bushy mustache dangled over his lip, making his tongue look like a slug squirming back and forth as he licked his lips. "Let you go?" he said in a heavy southern drawl. "We haven't even started yet."

Melanie cried, hating herself for it. Her tears made her vision blurry. She couldn't remember the last time she cried.

When Jon left for college. Watching him drive off got me going.

In private, in the bathroom, with the door shut. That way Harold couldn't see. He'd have really made an ordeal out of it.

Where are you, Harold?

Work. He'd left thirty minutes ago. Most days, he wasn't gone five minutes before he rushed back to get his cell phone. Always on the charger. He was usually in such a hurry that he'd walk out without it.

Had he forgotten it this morning?

The man between her legs leaned back on his knees. Legs folded under him, he put his hands flat on his thighs. He was staring at Melanie's robe, the pink cotton that was partially open. The slope of her left breast was exposed and that was where the man's eyes were focused.

Reaching out, he grabbed the edges of the robe and threw them wide, exposing both breasts. Pulling her eyes away from his hands, Melanie stared at the ceiling, trembling.

He's going to rape me. God, he's going to rape me and kill me. No way he'll let me live after seeing his face.

This wasn't her first time seeing his face. Yesterday morning, he'd rung the front doorbell. When she'd answered it, he'd claimed he was a landscaper looking for work. She'd noticed even then how his eyes had searched her, had searched over her shoulder, looking around at the two-story house she shared with Harold.

And she hadn't even told Harold about the guy coming by yesterday.

Wouldn't have mattered.

Harold would have nodded while reading the paper, pretending to listen but not really. That was what he did. Tuned her out. He conducted the marriage with blinders on, oblivious to everything that wasn't directly in front of him.

Or maybe he'd just grown so used to her complaining, he no longer heard it.

I still should've told him.

Something made a soft clicking sound in front of her. Looking above her breasts, Melanie saw the man had pulled out the blade of a very large pocketknife. The teeth on the bottom were sharp and seemed to shine under the light.

Melanie's breath quickened. Her stomach sucked in and shot out in quick flutters. Seeing this made the man's mouth arch into a strange half grin. He lowered the blade to her stomach. Feeling the cold kiss on her skin, Melanie held her breath. If she breathed, she might slice herself open.

The man turned the knife sideways, sliding it down her stomach. She felt the sharp point slip into her navel, then slide downward. It paused above her panties. She felt his hand twitching, like an anxious kid.

"Please," Melanie said again, not knowing what else to say. Then an idea hit her. "My husband...my husband!"

"What?" the man said.

"My husband." Her words were muffled behind the rag stuffed in her mouth. It was held there by the bandanna that had been on his head when she'd answered the door.

Such an idiot! Opened the door right up because I thought it was Harold!

"What about him?" the man asked.

"He'll be back any minute! He'll come home. He's big and strong and will...kick the shit out of you!" Melanie knew she sounded like a bratty little girl telling a bully about her big brother, but she didn't care. If the man believed her, maybe he'd think twice about doing what he was inevitably about to do.

The man threw back his head, laughed. He stayed that way for a good while, staring at the ceiling, his throat clucking. When he looked back down, he knuckled tears from his eyes. She saw shiny trails down his cheeks, vanishing in his thick beard. "Kick *my* ass?" He laughed again. "Oh, that's a good one. I saw your big and strong husband yesterday. Watched him leave, watched him leave this morning too. He won't be back until after five. And even if he did come home early, he can't kick my ass. Not that short, scrawny piece of shit. He'd get his ass handed to him by a child."

Melanie loosed deep, chest-heaving sobs. He was right. Harold wouldn't be able to help her. Even if he walked in right now, there would be nothing Harold could do to stop this. He'd probably be too scared to even attempt anything. The timid, shy guy she'd met in the library in her early twenties when she used to work there had been cute and sweet. It had worked for her then. Over the years, feelings changed on both sides. Harold made a ton of money at the software company he worked for, but he was not in any shape to be a physical threat to this man, or much of anybody.

"I like how your crying makes your tits jiggle. Damn them are some big titties." He grabbed one, squeezed it, shook it like somebody mixing an energy drink. "Sweet mercy." He whistled.

His touch sent sick tingles through her body. She felt her skin harden with gooseflesh. The man took a deep, quivery breath.

"You like it, don't you?" he asked.

"No…"

"Yeah, you do. You like it when ol' Ernest plays, huh?"

"No…"

Ernest laughed. He pinched her nipple, flattening it between his thumb and forefinger. Melanie sucked air through her nostrils. Snot fired down her throat, choking her. She coughed. Because of the gag, she couldn't get the air she needed to soothe the tickle in her throat. It felt as if she might swallow the rag. Forcing herself to breath slowly through her nose, she shut her eyes and let Ernest grope and paw her breasts. He moved down to her stomach, fingered her navel. He gripped the top of her panties.

And paused.

Melanie waited, recumbent and tensed, for him to delve. But he continued to wait.

"Thought I heard something…" he muttered. Sounded as if he was talking to himself more than Melanie.

Listening intently, Melanie hoped for any kind of sound. A car coming up the long driveway to their house, the soft crackles of tires on the gravel. Footsteps in the house. Maybe somebody from the power company was about to check their meter.

Do they even still do that?

She didn't know. Didn't matter, though. She didn't hear anything.

And Ernest must have been convinced he hadn't either. He ripped her panties open in one vicious yank. She felt the air of the room wash over her groin.

Ernest whistled. "Not shaved bald, but I like how you keep it trimmed." His fingers shoved into her.

Melanie jerked rigid, groaning behind the gag. She clamped her thighs around his hand. Not to keep him there. It had been an instant reaction. But Ernest laughed as if he thought she wanted his fingers inside.

"Hang on, lady," he said, laughing. "I'm ready too."

She felt the knife press against her belly. Slowly, she parted her thighs. He removed his fingers. The sounds of a zipper being lowered filled the room. It was so quiet in here, the soft taps of the zipper going down sounded like a chainsaw.

Melanie peaked an eye open. It looked as if Ernest was hatching from his navy-blue coveralls. His chest, pale and thick with orange fur, emerged from the gaping blue mouth of his clothes. He shoved the torso section down to his waist, pushed them lower.

He wore nothing underneath. His bloated penis dropped out, springy and stiff. Pale and long, it looked as if he'd coated it in grease. It shimmered in the light of the room.

That was going to be inside her.

Melanie wanted to kick him. But she knew if she flung her leg forward, his knife would punch into her side right above her hip. And even if she succeeded in knocking him off the bed, what could she do afterward? She was taped to the bed, heavily. She'd still be stuck when Ernest got up.

He'd punish her. A lot.

So she didn't resist when he patted her inner thighs. She spread them, wide enough for him to walk on his knees between them. She felt him prodding her, his penis hard and slick.

God, here it comes. He's going to do it.

He started to push. She felt her intimate ingress being pried open.

Then she heard a *whack!*

Ernest groaned. The bed popped as his weight shifted to the side. Opening her eyes, she saw the dazed expression on Ernest's face for a fleeting instant as it dropped sideways. He tumbled off the bed, hitting the floor with a heavy thud.

Harold stood at the foot of the bed, a fireplace poker over his shoulder as if he'd just knocked a baseball out of the park. To Melanie, he had. He'd nailed the ball good.

"Harold!" she cried behind the gag. It hit her tongue, gagging her.

If her petite husband had heard her, he gave no indication. He stared off to the side, where Ernest had most likely landed. Lowering the poker, he rubbed his mouth with the back of his hand. It was a habit of his. Whenever he was nervous, he wiped his mouth over and over. He was doing this now, unable to stop as he stared at the product of his actions.

"Harold!"

This time he heard her, for sure. He turned, glanced at her eyes, then looked down. She watched his eyes start at her breasts and work down to her groin that showed between the tattered curtains of her panties.

His hand went back to his mouth, rubbing.

"Harold!" Melanie called for a third time.

Blinking, Harold shook his head. "Melanie!" He ran around the other side of the bed, sitting at her hip. "Are you all right?"

Melanie started to answer, remembered the gag, and stopped. She tilted her head to the side, widening her eyes.

Harold caught the hint. "Oh!" He leaned over her, setting the poker by her side. Then he reached behind her head, fumbling with the knot. Sometimes he accidentally pulled her hair, causing her to wince. She felt the knot drop away. "Sorry," he said. Bet it's hard to talk with this in your mouth.

Melanie worked with her tongue to shove the rag forward. As she felt it touching her teeth, Harold reached out, grimacing as he plucked the rag free. Melanie took a deep breath. "Harold..." She took another deep breath. It felt good to breathe without the rag clogging her mouth. She could still taste it. "I'm so glad you...came home."

Harold made a dopey smile. Shrugged. "Forgot my phone again."

For once, she was thankful that he had.

"I came in and heard him talking about your..." He looked at her breasts. "Those. Then I snuck to the fireplace, grabbed the poker, and came back."

So Ernest had heard something: Harold sneaking around the house for a weapon. Melanie was certain her surprise showed on her face.

"He couldn't see me coming in because his back was to the door." Harold pointed at the door as if she didn't know where it was located. "Guess you didn't see me, either."

"No." She tried to wiggle her arms. The tape held them firmly in place. "Now stop yapping about it and get me loose."

"I should call the police."

"Get me loose first, damn it."

Harold closed his eyes, sighed. Same thing he always did when she started yelling. "Mel. Now's not the time to raise your voice. I just saved your life."

Melanie opened her mouth to remind Harold that she was about to be raped and probably killed and that her demeanor was completely understandable, given the situation. But she held the words in. She let out a long breath. "Just get a knife and cut me loose. Now?"

Harold nodded. "Fine."

"Wait," she said. "He had a knife. It should be around here somewhere."

Harold stood, walked around to the foot of the bed. "Ah." He bent over, vanishing. Felt like he was down there for five minutes before he straightened, holding the knife and giving her that same impish grin. "Found it."

"Good."

She noticed his eyes had lowered between her legs. She closed them, feeling a slimy flow make its way up her body. Harold looked her in the eye.

"Is he dead?" she asked, trying to distract him from her covering herself. She shouldn't feel odd being naked in front of Harold, but she always had.

She knew she had a nice body, but she liked to keep it covered, even around her husband. It was how he looked at her, made her feel…awkward.

Harold checked the side of the bed again. "He's breathing. Bet he won't be moving around anytime soon. The back of his head is cracked open. Bleeding a lot."

"That's what he gets."

Harold smiled. He started around the side of the bed again. She glimpsed the front of his jutting pants. *My God, he's hard!* Melanie wanted to ask him what was so arousing about this, but didn't. She smiled when he sat down.

Harold leaned over her, raising the knife to her hand. "Wow, he really made this tight, didn't he?"

"Yeah. I can hardly feel my arms anymore."

"I'll have you free in a jiff."

"Good. Just do it, already. But don't slice me open."

"You know…" Harold lowered his arms, leaned back so he could look at her. "I've never seen you so…" He held his hand up, as if he might grab the word he wanted out of the air.

"So, what?"

"Um…vulnerable."

"Why is that thought occurring to you?"

"It just is." He stared at her, clucking his tongue. "I'm right, though. Usually you're in the position to give all the orders, but it's kind've hard for you right now, isn't it?"

"Harold."

"I'm just stating it, Mel. That's all."

"Yes," she forced herself to say. She even got a smile to form. "I guess you're right."

"You don't like it, do you?"

"Cut..."

"Do you?"

She couldn't believe what she was hearing. Where were these inappropriate questions coming from? "No, Harold. I don't like it."

"It's because you're naked, isn't it? You don't like me seeing your body."

Though he was right again, she shook her head as if he was being silly. "That's not true."

"How many times have I seen you naked?"

"When we make love."

"At night? With the lights off?" He shook his head, clucking his tongue again. "No. I think really the only times are when I purposely walk in on you in the shower and..."

"I knew it," she said. "Creep."

"Mel. Really? Name calling? Right now?"

"I'm sorry, I'm just...worked up."

"I bet."

"What's that supposed to mean?"

"I didn't forget my phone," he said. "I was watching you."

Melanie's back felt as if it was being scratched with icy claws as she watched him pull his phone from his pocket, play with the screen. He held it up to her. On the small display, she saw a bird's eye view of Ernest pulling her robe apart.

She looked up at the ceiling. The light was a decorative mock-chandelier, dangling from a short length of imitation gold chain. Somewhere up there, Harold had hidden a camera.

"I wanted to see what you do in here when I'm not home."

"You goddamn pervert!"

"Again with the name calling." He shook his head. "You talk to yourself quite a bit."

Melanie cringed inside. She talked to herself about Harold all the time, so it was hard to know just what he'd heard her say.

"You don't think very highly of me," he said, "do you?"

"It's just me talking, Harold…that's all."

"Shut up!" He jabbed the side of her thigh with the knife. Then he jumped back, gasping at what he'd done.

Melanie screamed. The knife hadn't gone in very deep, but it still burned as if a fire had been lit in her muscle. Really, her explosive reaction came from the realization her husband had just *stabbed* her.

"Holy Moley!" Harold shouted.

"You stabbed me?" Melanie screamed. "You…stabbed *me?*"

"I didn't mean to…"

"Yes, you did!" Melanie's sobs turned to loud wails. She watched Harold through her tear-soaked eyes, pacing back and forth, his hands covering his ears.

"Stop it!" he shouted.

Melanie didn't stop, she got louder. She knew how he hated being yelled at and she was really letting herself go now.

"I said stop!" he yelled, trying to be louder than her. But he couldn't. She knew it, and he knew it. "Stop!"

Melanie kept on. She almost smiled because she knew how much it was bothering him. But her smile died at birth when she saw him stripping out of his clothes. Her scream petered off to a whine. "Harold? What are you...?"

He climbed onto the bed, his erection pointing at her. He was naked except for his knee-high black socks.

"Wait," she said. "Don't...Harold. What do you think you're going to do?"

"With the lights on, that's what." He pushed his way between her legs, crawling forward.

She kicked, threw her feet out, but he was already up too far. Her resistance was useless. "Stop it!" she cried, now sounding like Harold had a short while ago. "Please don't...do this."

"I'm doing it," he said. He dropped on top of her, his mouth finding a nipple. It was the same one Ernest had been twisting. He flicked it with his tongue a few times before looking up at her. Saliva made a wet ring around his mouth. "You really do have a nice body; you shouldn't hide it from me."

Before she could say anything, he shoved into her.

As Melanie screamed and begged for him to stop, Harold thrust violently until he was done.

Melanie stared at the ceiling. She felt numb everywhere but between her legs. Harold's seed trickled out, running down her thigh. She was sore inside, throbbing. She no longer felt the pain in her leg from the knife, only the heat inside of her, like a dull fire that wouldn't go out.

Above her, she heard bumping sounds, followed by something being dragged across the floor. Harold had taken Ernest up there, to Jon's room. She wasn't sure why.

Before Harold had squirted inside her, she'd already decided she wouldn't do anything about this. She figured when he finished, he would return to his senses and let her go. Then they could call the cops. He'd spend the rest of their lives making it up to her.

But he hadn't done any of those things. When he'd finished, he'd gone straight into their bathroom. She'd heard him showering through the closed door. He'd even whistled a melody as he'd cleaned himself. He'd come out a few minutes later, in his robe, smiling.

After bandaging her leg, he'd walked over to Ernest, grabbed his feet, and dragged him away.

She stared at the ceiling some more, realized it was quiet up there. Then the sound of Harold's footfalls came from the hallway. He was heading to the kitchen.

A good while later, Harold returned to the room. A tray was balanced on his hand. On top, she saw a sandwich and a tall glass of orange juice with a bendy straw draped over the rim. Her mouth watered as she stared at the orange fluid.

"Hungry?" he asked. "Thirsty? I want to make sure you stay hydrated. We've got a few days ahead of us and you'll need your energy."

Melanie's stomach folded in on itself, robbing her of her appetite. Though she'd hated to admit it, until now, even after what Harold had done to her, she'd been very hungry.

Harold sat down on the edge of the bed, lowering the tray to his lap. "It's ham and turkey, your favorite."

"Why are you doing this to me? You're my husband. You're..." She shook her head. "You're no different than Ernest."

"That's his name?"

"Yes. You're no different than he is."

"I'm nothing like him."

"You...*raped* me, Harold. Your own wife." Her voice turned thick. Tears wetted the corners of her eyes. Before today, Harold had never seen her cry. Even when her mother had been killed in a car accident, she hadn't cried in front of Harold.

Instead of showing any hints of shame, Harold just smiled. "I guess I got a little crazy, didn't I?"

"A little...crazy?"

"You know what I was on my way to do this morning?" Melanie stared at him. "I was going to throw myself in front of a train. I left a note on the fridge, but I saw it was still under the magnet. I know you went into the kitchen at least three times before Ernest showed up."

"I didn't see it." And she hadn't, really. Sure, she'd opened the fridge each time she'd gone in there, but she hadn't been looking for a note so naturally she hadn't seen one. "Honest, Harold."

"See? You're doing it again. Instead of asking me why I wanted to kill myself, you're trying to make yourself out to be in the right about the note."

Had she been doing that?

"I'm…I didn't mean to."

"Still can't even say you're sorry. Even now." Harold groaned. "Wow. I was going to kill myself because I was tired of it all. My job, my life, living with a wife who hated me."

"You put up cameras in the house!"

"Really, it started off innocently. I just wanted to know more about you. We've been married for over twenty years, and I still don't know much about you. I wanted to see what you were like when I wasn't around. Then I started enjoying watching you, you know? Sometimes you'd shower, then come out in the bedroom with nothing on. Get dressed. Only one time did you ever play with yourself. I was surprised by that. Figured you did it all the time when I wasn't around."

"Let me go, Harold. Let's call the police, have them take Ernest away, then we can put this behind us, okay? We both know there are…issues in the marriage that need to be addressed. We can take care of that."

"Tempting, but no. I'm leaving you there."

Tears streamed down her face. "Why!?!" She flung herself against the mattress. "Damn it, why?"

Harold smiled again. "Because I like you where you are. When I saw Ernest on my phone, forcing you to get on the bed, I got really worried about you at first. But I noticed how quickly you submitted to him."

"He had a knife!"

"You didn't know that at first. You let him force his way in, force you in here and tape you up. You answered the door in your robe!"

"I thought it was you!"

"You never answer the door in your robe when you know it's me."

"I…" Melanie stopped. She wasn't sure why she'd gone to the door in a robe, wearing only her panties underneath. She'd just showered and had been comfortable. That was all. There'd been no thought to it.

"Let's not talk about it anymore and ruin our lunch," Harold said, "okay?"

"Harold…this has to stop."

"It will. When I'm ready for it to. Since I'd planned on dying today, I told my job I was going out of town. Took the week off and cashed in my vacation pay. It's in a bag on my backseat. That was for you. I wanted to make sure you got it. But now my plan's changed. I want to have some fun for a while. Got to make sure you eat, so when I call the police later this week to report you were murdered, they'll believe me. See, you have food in your system, shows we spent time together."

Melanie shivered. Harold was going to kill her? *Kill* her? "You won't get away with it, Harold. Please, just let me go before you go too far."

"I thought it out while I was in the shower. You know I get my best ideas in the shower. I'm going to keep Ernest tied up upstairs. Then I'm going to bring him down here when I'm ready. Kill you, then kill him. I'll say I walked in on him finishing you off.

Fought with him and managed to kill him, then the grieving husband will handle all the funeral arrangements. And that hefty life insurance policy will give me more than enough money to retire on. A new life can begin. Exciting, no?"

Melanie stared at the man she'd been living with for almost twenty-five years. And for the first time, she realized she'd been married to a stranger. He was going to kill her; there was no talking him out of it.

"Now, let's eat. Got to get that energy built up."

After lunch, he climbed on top of her again. He was much rougher this time.

"Come on, Mel," said Harold. "Smile."

"Fuck off."

Harold laughed. With his head on her shoulder, he held his phone above their faces. "Come on. We can't be spending time together if we're not taking pictures of it, right? That's what happy couples do, isn't it? Now smile."

Melanie stuck out her tongue. Harold snapped the picture. The flash lit up the room. It had gotten dark outside, and the only light came from the lamp on the nightstand table.

Chuckling, Harold sat up. He stared at the screen. "Perfect. Even better than I expected. Love the tongue. They'll think you're being playful. And you can't even tell you're naked."

Melanie stared down at herself. Her nipples were swollen from two days' worth of Harold's biting and pinching. But her skin looked soft and shiny in the dim lamplight. He'd used a basin of warm, soapy water and a washcloth to bathe her. He'd even washed between her legs. She'd recognized the soap's scent as hers from the bathroom.

"Have to make sure you're cleaned every day," he'd said. "That way when they take traces of your body, it'll show you've been using your soap."

The amount of detail he'd put into his plan in such a short amount of time was frightening.

Maybe it wasn't such a short time. Maybe he'd been trying to think of a way to kill me for a long time now and was too scared to try, until an opportunity like this came along.

Her husband hated her. And now that she'd realized it, she also realized she felt nothing about it. Maybe if he'd just told her out of the blue, over dinner one night, the impact would have been more catastrophic.

What surprised her more was she hated her husband back. Maybe she always had. Would explain why she'd treated him so poorly for so many years. Thinking back on it now, she'd treated him as if he were the village idiot, a man-sized child. Usually, she reminded him of this in front of people.

Such a bitch, at times.

So what! And that gets me this!

She tried tugging at the layers of tape. Her arms didn't budge. Her shoulders didn't budge. She couldn't feel them. It was as if her arms had been severed. She hoped there wouldn't be any kind of permanent damage, then decided it didn't matter. She wasn't getting out of here.

Letting her head drop on the pillow, she stared at the ceiling. Jon's room was right above her. Ernest was in there. He'd yelled a few times earlier, so that meant he was very much alive. Harold went up there and muffled him somehow. At times, she could hear him grunting through the ceiling, or some banging that she assumed came from him stomping on the floor. Harold must not have put him on the bed. Probably couldn't lift him. Harold wasn't necessarily strong. Getting him up there probably had been a feat he'd barely managed to accomplish.

Closing her eyes, Melanie hoped sleep would come quickly, putting another day of this nightmare behind her, another day closer to her death. She wondered if she should feel upset about that. Probably. But she wasn't exactly feeling much of anything other than betrayal.

Just as she was starting to doze off, her bladder nudged her. Melanie began to cry, knowing she'd have to call for Harold to bring her a bowl. It was the bowl that had come from her grandmother. She'd used it to mix up cookie batter and that was what Melanie used it for also. Worse than the humiliation of Harold holding it between her legs and wiping her when she was done was knowing that her family heirloom was ruined.

Melanie sucked her sobs down, took many gulps, and let out a long breath.

Then she called for Harold.

Voices shocked Melanie awake.

The room was heavy in darkness, only a meager silvery glow managed to push through the thick curtains.

Laughing. And not just Harold. She heard somebody else.

A girl.

"Oh, you are a tiger, aren't you?" she said between chortles.

"I'm learning more about myself every day," said Harold.

For some reason, this statement elicited a wild round of squeaky laughter from the girl. Melanie heard footfalls coming toward the bedroom.

"Are you sure she won't mind?" the girl asked.

"Not at all. I told you—it's her fantasy."

What the hell's going on now?

The door swung open. The light switch clicked, and the room was blasted with light that hurt Melanie's eyes. Harold entered, smiling. He looked down at Melanie and his smile fell away slightly. "Awake?"

"What do you think?" she asked in a raspy voice. Her throat felt as if she'd gargled with cotton—dry and sore.

Harold, still giving her that smile, nodded. "Let me get you some water." He stepped out of the room. Melanie could hear the girl whispering something to him. "It's fine. She's thirsty. Give us a few minutes. Make yourself comfortable in my office."

"Okay."

"It's right over there," he said.

"I see it," said the girl in a sing-song voice, making her sound even younger. Laughing, her feet made prancing taps on the floor as she dashed away. "Mind if I snort some of this?"

Harold was quiet a moment before saying, "If that's what you like to do, then so be it."

The girl, who sounded more like a bubbly teenager, laughed.

Harold brings a girl into our home? And she's on drugs?

Was Harold suffering some kind of mental crisis? It made sense, kind of. Now he was getting out of control.

Harold returned a short while later with a glass of water and another folding straw hooked on the rim. "Here," he said, sitting.

Melanie raised her head, forming her lips around the straw. She ignored Harold's aroused stare as he watched her drink. Though she wanted to guzzle the water, she knew better. Last time, she'd nearly drowned herself. She took slow, heavy gulps. When the glass was halfway empty, she pulled back.

Harold set the glass on her nightstand.

"What have you done now?" she asked.

"Are you talking about Starla?"

"Starla?" Harold nodded. "That's her name?" Another nod. "What is she, a prostitute?"

"Something of the sort."

Melanie should have been shocked, but she wasn't. "You brought a whore into our house?"

Nose wrinkled, Harold pressed his lips tightly together. "Not a nice word, dear. A paid companion is a much gentler, and appropriate, term."

Melanie, mouth gaping, couldn't speak. She made coughing sounds as she tried to force the words out.

Standing, Harold began pacing alongside the bed. "This may sound crazy, but please hear me out. I was thinking about it last night and at first I couldn't believe I was even considering it, but you know what? The more I thought it out, the more it just made sense to me." He stopped pacing, turned to face Melanie. "I'm going to have sex with her while you watch."

"Harold!"

"It's okay. I told her you're into it. She likes women too, so it should be really fun. I told her it was okay to mess around with you, too."

There was a loud banging sound from deep in the house.

Harold spun around, a look of concern on his face. Now he looked like the man she'd known all these years as he ran out of the room.

Melanie listened as Harold called for Starla. Starting off playful, his tone quickly turned urgent. Then there was a beat of silence before Harold shouted.

Melanie's skin went prickly. Something was wrong. Something had happened that Harold hadn't prepared for during one of his shower planning sessions.

The bedroom door flung wide. Harold entered, eyes wide and roaming, mouth opened into a pained grimace.

"What's wrong?" she asked behind the gag.

Harold paused just inside the room, looking this way and that. "She's dead."

Melanie shivered. She knew who he was talking about.

"Throat slit in the living room. Looked like she was robbing us when somebody…" He shook his head. "She had a bag with things from my office stuffed inside.

"She's dead?"

Harold nodded. His eyes snapped wide. "Ernest!" He charged out of the room. She heard him running through the house, the pounding of his shoes on the stairs at the end of the hall. The ceiling began to creak and groan as he moved up to the second-floor hall.

Ernest's loose!

Though Harold hadn't confirmed it, Melanie knew it was true. When Harold yelled above her, she knew it for certain. She didn't know how he'd gotten free, nor did she care. Fact of the matter—he was loose in the house!

Melanie jerked her arms back and forth. The tape held. Each movement sent static-like pain through her arms. Her hands were numb.

There was a loud crash above her that shook the house. The overhead light swayed, throwing bouncy streaks across the walls that reminded Melanie of the sun reflecting off a lake. The chains holding the light jingled quietly.

Harold grunted. A muffled smacking sound followed. Another crash, things clattered. She heard a sweeping tumble start on one side and work its way to the other. Somebody was being dragged.

They're fighting.

Harold screamed. His screams turned to hollers of pain as they began to fade. Just below those sounds was another: the unremitting wet punching that carried on well after Harold's screams had stopped.

From outside, crickets chirped, their melodies drifting into the house. It seemed odd and out of place, such a peaceful backdrop to the violence that had just happened upstairs.

The soft thump of Jon's door closing came through the ceiling. Lethargic footsteps followed, making their way to the stairs, then down them. Melanie held her breath, listened. The steps stopped when they reached the floor.

Faintly, she heard the huffs of heavy breathing.

Then the footsteps started up again, heading her way.

Melanie nearly attempted another go at getting her arms free. There was no use. Ernest had done too great of a job at winding the tape. She was stuck here. No place to go, nothing to do, but wait for him to enter.

And he did, a few moments later. Still dressed in his navy-blue coveralls, he walked into the room. His beard looked mussed and tangled. He had a black eye, and it looked as if his head had been bandaged. She wondered if he'd done that himself at some point, or Harold had done it.

In his hand was Jon's hunting knife. Though Jon had only gone hunting a few times, he'd wanted the knife. It had a large blade, bowed tip for wrenching out entrails. It was soaked in blood, as was Ernest's hand. His sleeve was streaked in dark, wet lines. She even noticed some spattered patterns on his face and brow that had turned pink from his sweat.

Shoulders rising and dropping, Ernest looked around the room. His eyes moved all over, scanning. They came to a stop on her. This time, he looked her in the eye.

"Anybody else sneaking around the house?" he asked in a winded voice.

Melanie shook her head.

"You're sure?"

She nodded.

"All right." He stepped over to the bed, switching the knife to his other hand. He stroked her thigh. "There it is…" He took a deep breath. "What say we start back where we left off, now that there won't be any more interruptions."

Melanie wanted to cry, *wished* she could cry. But there was nothing left inside. She felt numb as Ernest climbed onto the bed.

Story Notes:

Probably the darkest one of the bunch. I'd had the idea for this story for a long time, but I always thought it would be longer, maybe a novella. I was asked to contribute to a German anthology that was being edited by one of my favorites, Edward Lee, for German publisher, Festa-Verlag. They took the German rights, and I held onto the English rights, thinking I might not ever release it anywhere in the states. Sometimes, my stories get ripped apart for their violence, and I wondered if this one might have taken things a bit too far. It didn't take long before I decided to get over myself and stop worrying about it. The story is just fine, and I like it a lot. I don't feel *too* guilty for writing it.

GEARHART'S WIFE

John Gearhart.
No way it's the same guy.

But how many John Gearharts could there possibly be? Sure, the first name was very ordinary, but how common could the last name possibly be? Gearhart. And how many people could possibly have *both* names, and not be the one Tobe hoped him to be.

Tobe Crooks couldn't think of anyone else other than *the* John Gearhart, the man who'd directed a bale of exploitation movies in the late seventies before graduating to gory splatter movies in the eighties. ·

The only John Gearhart he'd ever heard of.

What am I gonna do if the door opens and it's actually him?

Probably piss his pants, and spend another hour awkwardly apologizing for the ammonia-like smell while the horror legend signed his home refinance papers.

That was Tobe's job—taking paperwork from title companies to the borrowers to be signed, then notarizing their signatures to make it legal. He was frequently introduced to an array of houses and living conditions and not one of them was ever identical. *And the pets!* Tobe liked pets, his family even owned some, but he'd been in some houses where the pets were running the lot, and not the owners. There was one evening where he'd been subjected to having to watch a toddler roll around on the floor in cat puke stains. As much as he'd wanted to ask how they could let their kid play in filth and cat excrement, he couldn't say a word. It was his job to go in, smile, and no matter what the environment was, he had to represent the lending companies in a positive light.

A glorified paperboy who had to suck it up and shut up.

He'd been doing the job for over a year now, and this was the most excitement he'd experienced. The possibility of meeting one of his favorites in the genre, a true icon in the horror world. His stomach buzzed with anxiety, a nice change from his drab work routine. He felt like all he did anymore was drive, stop at gas stations long enough to pump a small fortune into the tank, buy a cherry Dr. Pepper and some kind of beef jerky, and then drive some more. To say he was getting tired of it was a meek interpretation.

Typically, when he was at home his family wasn't. His three kids would be in school, his wife at work, leaving it his responsibility to be the housekeeper since Kaylyn had to handle all the evening parental duties herself. He often became lonely, cranky, and his temper's fuse was about as long as a grass seed. The job had lost its new car smell, and he needed to swap out the car fresheners almost daily.

He'd had a love for horror movies for as long as he could remember. But he wasn't exactly sure when it began. It'd just always been there. He'd even contemplated a career making his own films. It had been easier when he was younger to take a video camera and a group of friends into the woods to record some kind of short, gory picture. It had been a lot of fun. Eventually, his friends lost interest. And without the motivation his friends had offered and the support they'd given him, his desire to make horror movies quickly diminished. His parents had been encouraging enough while he was growing up, but as he got older, inspirational talks became less about the art of making movies and more about the security of growing up and getting a *real* job.

He slowed the Jeep as he neared a four-way intersection.

"In point-seven miles, turn right onto Windy Circle Drive," said the husky, android-like voice of the GPS. He'd named her Felicia, for no reason other than he thought she sounded like one.

His stomach cramped.

Almost there.

The drive had been agonizingly long, yet had seemed to zip by too quickly. Checking the clock on the console, he saw he'd been driving for just over an hour and was almost to the destination. He wasn't prepared. He needed to figure out what he was going to say without coming off as a weirdo fan-boy. Tobe was going to be in *his* house and if this was *the* John Gearhart, then he would probably be skeptical of having someone who knew who he was in his home and having such intimate access to all his personal information. He might even think Tobe had somehow intentionally planned this.

But if it was *the* John Gearhart, what was he doing in North Carolina? Tobe knew at one point he'd resided in Georgia, which was where the majority of his films took place. He supposed he could have moved. It had been nearly fifteen years since the man had made a movie, so it was very plausible that he'd retired from the movie business and settled here.

The GPS reminded him his turn was forthcoming, so he slowed the car down, checking his mirrors for cars. He saw none, nor had he seen any in a good while. It had been only his car on this stretch of blacktop with nothing but countryside all around.

Tobe steered the Jeep into Windy Circle and stopped at the mouth of the gravel road. It sketched through the woods and looked as if it might go on forever. Was this the right place? He put the car in park, and double checked the address on the confirmation sheet he'd gotten from the title company.

111 Windy Circle Drive.

Tobe checked the faded wooden sign sitting at an angle along the side of the road. The names matched. This was the right place.

He rolled the window down. It had recently rained, and the late spring air outside was thick and sticky. With his head poking out through the open space, he looked from right to left. He'd expected to find a plank of mailboxes, or possibly a stake with house numbers nailed to it, but he found nothing other than the aging road sign.

Maybe this is his driveway. Not a road.

The GPS showed him the distance left to travel was two miles. On the screen were thick green blotches around the purple line for the road that suggested woodland would barricade him once he drove inward.

Sighing, Tobe put the Jeep in gear, and started forward. He left the window down, enjoying the wind brushing his cheek and the sweet smell of the damp woods. He could hear gravel popping under his tires.

As he traveled, the woods seemed to close in around the Jeep, pressing tighter on him as if the limbs wanted to reach in and snatch him out. He stared at the leafy, low-hanging branches. He supposed they did resemble big green hands. Although he knew they wouldn't start groping at him, he rolled up the window.

The air coming from the vents suddenly felt too cold on his dampening skin. He could feel the inklings of a chill squirming up his spine. He turned the AC down low. Then he noticed the house marker, its golden numbers twinkling in the shadowed area under the trees. *111*. He kept on, following the gravel road through the woods.

Finally, the path opened up on a two story, log cabin-style home with a wall of woods behind it. The trees crowded around the wooden structure, their thick arms held out as if trying to keep anyone from seeing the house behind them. There was a decent-sized yard in the back, neatly cut grass on each side, and a three-door garage sitting off to the left that wasn't connected to the house. A Ford Escape was parked at an angle in front.

It was a cozy, yet capacious place. Just the kind of home Tobe had always dreamed of owning himself. He parked the Jeep behind the Escape and twisted the key, killing the engine. He patted his pocket to make sure his cell phone was in there. It was. Then he grabbed his briefcase from the back seat and stepped out of the car.

The air felt like a heated moist blanket on his skin. The chills he'd had were gone, and now he could feel sweat under his shirt. If he started sweating, he wouldn't stop. Hopefully John Gearhart, whether he was the one he hoped he was or not, had air-conditioning cranked to high.

Sunlight reflected off the beads of dew dotting the grass. Tobe could see mist curling along the trees, making its way into the yard as evening approached and brought cooler temperatures with it. He quickly crossed the graveled driveway, and climbed the wooden steps to the porch. An eave was above him and followed the length of the porch around to the side of the house. Planters hung from hooks with vibrantly colored vines growing out of them. He'd never seen such plants before and wondered what they were. Kaylyn liked to dabble in gardening, but usually that entailed the slow slaughter of credulous plant breeds. These that hung all around were lovely flora, and he'd like to have some decorating their house.

Tobe used his index finger to ring the doorbell. He could hear the faint chime reverberating within the house. He looked around as he waited. There were two rocking chairs, a small table set up between them with an ash tray on top and a half-smoked cigar nestled in the corner.

The sound of footsteps approaching the door came from the other side. The back of his throat felt as if it were bubbling. *No way* would this play out how he'd hoped. Still, he couldn't stop himself from being anxious about it.

A lock clicked.

Tobe's heart hammered.

Another lock clicked.

He readied himself for disappointment.

Then the doorknob turned, and the door swayed inward. A shape appeared in the shroud of shadows behind the mesh of the screen door. Standing on the other side was a man, an older man, probably in his late seventies. Other than some worry lines around his eyes, he appeared to be very healthy for his age. His face looked smooth and wholesome. He had a short moustache above his lip, sugar-colored hair, and thick black glasses that reminded Tobe of the digital 3D glasses from the movie theaters.

Tobe smiled. He'd seen enough pictures of the filmmaker and had watched plenty of interviews on special-edition DVDs to be certain.

This was *him*!

"Yes," Gearhart said.

"Mr. Gearhart?"

"That's me."

"Hi, I'm Tobe."

"The Mobile Notary, I presume."

"That's *me.*"

"Great," he pushed open the screen door. "Come on in."

Gearhart stepped back to give him room for entrance. Tobe entered the house, taking the door from him, and letting it bang shut behind him. From the brightness outside, stepping into the house was like entering a cave. His eyes had trouble adjusting to the sudden change in luminosity.

Tobe gave the foyer a quick scan. Nothing about the interior design screamed a horror movie legend lived here, and he assumed that was because of the wife. She was the one who'd probably chosen the decor.

"Where should we do this?" asked John Gearhart.

"Oh—uh anywhere there's a flat surface. A table would be best."

Nodding, Gearhart pointed up the hall to a pair of French doors on the right. "Would the dining room work for you?"

"Oh, that's fine. Whatever's easiest for you, I'm game."

Gearhart smiled. "Good. Follow me."

Tobe was led to the doors. Gearhart pushed them open, unveiling a dining room on the other side. A china cabinet was at the back of the room, a small writing desk in a corner, and a long oval table in the middle with six chairs surrounding it. The rest of the room was empty.

"Have a seat," he said.

Tobe nodded as he approached the table, carefully sitting his scuffed briefcase on top. It wasn't made of leather, or even padded on the inside. His was much too cheap for that and had been built of proclaimed, durable plastic. He feared it might scratch the table's glossy surface, so he removed it and put it on the floor beside the chair at the head of the table.

Tobe wanted to talk about Gearhart's movies, wanted to tell him he was an admirer of his work. He was wary of how the legend might react.

Just tell him.

What if he got upset? Tobe could picture Gearhart's pleasant face fuming red. *"I can't get away from this kind of pestering, even in my own home!"*

Tobe sighed.

Gearhart noticed. "Everything okay?" He was about to sit at the chair diagonal from Tobe.

He nodded. "Yeah…it's just that…"

After a few seconds passed, Gearhart spoke up. "Just that what?" He was smiling again. It was almost as if he knew what Tobe wanted to say.

"When I got the confirmation email for this closing…I recognized your name…"

"Oh?" Still smiling.

"Yeah. And I wasn't sure if it was *actually* you or not. I mean…well…"

A few more seconds passed, then Gearhart advocated, "Go on."

Sighing again, Tobe said, "I'm a *huge* admirer of your work. I've even read your film-making books and the entire library of horror novels you've written."

"Have you now?"

Tobe nodded.

"Hmmm…" Gearhart scratched his chin. "So, when you took this closing and saw my name you probably thought there was no way it could be the *same* John Gearhart."

"That's *exactly* what I thought."

"And when I opened the door you saw it really was me?"

"That's pretty much the gist of it."

"Ah." He placed his hands on the back of the chair. "No wonder you gasped when I opened the door."

"I gasped?" Tobe felt himself blush.

Gearhart nodded. "I thought there was something wrong with my face." He chuckled.

Which brought a soft laugh from Tobe. "I'm sorry if I'm imposing on you by pointing out how much I respect your work. I just had to say it."

"You're not imposing on me at all. I'm flattered."

"Thank God."

Gearhart laughed. Not his polite chuckle, but an actual guffaw. "I haven't made a movie in quite a long time, so knowing somebody remembers me at all is a *wonderful* thing."

"A lot of people remember you. There're message boards devoted to you. A lot of posts are hopeful that you'll return to the director's chair."

"Is that a fact?"

"I wouldn't lie about it."

"Wow. I've been thinking about it…just can't seem to work up the, uh…"

Now Gearhart was cursed by long pauses. "Motivation?" Tobe offered.

Gearhart nodded. "Something along those lines, yes. I just don't have the drive these days. Plus, I'm not as young as I used to be."

"Please...you could get tons of young folks like me to help you with the work so you can just direct the movie..."

"Oh?"

Shut up, Tobe. Now you're imposing.

"You make movies?" Gearhart asked.

Tobe debated telling him, but went ahead and did so. "I used to...years back. Nothing serious. Just some shorts..."

"Were they good?"

"People said so."

Actually, he'd been told so many times he had a natural gift for scaring people, that he should be making features, he'd started to believe it himself.

"Real people? Or friends?"

Tobe laughed. "Real people. We did some screenings at auditoriums and places like that. I even printed out some questionnaires for people to answer and left a blank spot for people to write their own criticisms. Usually the most flack I got were the actors' inabilities to, well...act."

They both laughed.

Gearhart cleared his throat. "I've received some of those same criticisms myself. I remember when *Flesh Butcher* was released in 1980, the initial reviews were positive for the most part, but they didn't like the lead actress."

"Marylyn Palmers?"

"That's her. I should've known better than to cast an adult star as my lead actress."

"I thought she did okay."

He shrugged. "She wasn't bad I guess, but I was more worried about box-office sales than what the critics had to say, and I knew she would attract a...*broader*...audience. Or so I thought."

"Did she?"

"She did. But I speculate now if it was the kind of audience I should have wanted." He laughed. "My wife Glenda was not pleased with me casting her."

Tobe had read several interviews of Gearhart's and he *never* failed to mention his wife. It was obvious he truly loved her, and that had always made Tobe smile, knowing that a couple who'd been married as long as they had were still so happy.

"I'm sure my wife wouldn't have approved either," Tobe said.

Gearhart's eyebrows lifted. "You're married?"

Tobe nodded.

"That's wonderful! How long"

"Ten years."

"Wow, you got married young, huh?"

"Yeah, we weren't even old enough to drink yet."

"That is young. Was she pregnant?"

Tobe shook his head, laughing. "No. We get asked that a lot."

"I bet so. *Do* you have kids?"

"Yep. Three."

"That's wonderful. We never had kids. Kept putting it off, then one day we realized we were too old to try."

It always made Tobe uncomfortable when people made penitent statements like that. He never knew how to respond, and this time was no different. So he only nodded.

There was silence for a few more seconds, then Gearhart smiled. "Want to see some cool stuff before we get started?"

Tobe nearly shrieked with delight. "What kind of cool stuff?"

"Come on." He motioned with his hand. "You'll love it."

He all but ran over to where Gearhart was.

Tobe followed him out of the dining room. They made their way to the end of the hall. When Tobe had first looked down this way, he'd thought this was a wall, but now that he was closer, he realized it was actually a door. The handle was a latch, not a knob, and there were framed photos of people hanging on it. They all looked to be posing for the camera. He figured they were, in all probability, family members, although they more resembled models pretending to be enjoying a day of sailing.

Gearhart tugged the door open, then flicked the light switch next to the paneling. A dim light clicked on.

"Mind the first step," Gearhart said, stepping through the opening. He continued shrinking until Tobe could no longer see him.

When Tobe stepped through the door, he saw that Gearhart hadn't been reducing in size but was actually descending a set of carpeted stairs. He could see a section of matching carpet down at the bottom. Gearhart was already out of sight.

Tobe quickly went down.

He stood at the aperture of a small theater. He counted five rows of movie seats arranged stadium-style, and a large projection screen built into the wall. He slowly moved forward, looking around. There was a 35mm film projector assembled on a wooden crate at the back of the room, and shelves of film reels beside it. The walls couldn't be seen behind the posters, lobby cards, and various newspaper ads that wallpapered one side to another. He saw full-sized theatrical one-sheets and smaller 11x17 posters, some with monsters and others depicting scantily clad damsels shrieking in repulsed horror at whatever was pursuing them.

All of them were from Gearhart's movies.

"Like it?" he heard the man ask.

Tobe turned and saw Gearhart standing next to a life-sized prop display of the Sasquatch monster from Gearhart's movie, *'Quatch*. Not trusting his voice enough to answer the question, he nodded.

"There's more through there," he nodded toward a single, narrow doorway on the other side of the room.

Tobe wanted to see what was in there, but he had to move at a more cautious speed, since his legs had gone wobbly. He'd never seen such an amazing presentation of movie history. Sure, all of it was centered on Gearhart, but usually he had to go online and search images to see the kind of memorabilia that was spread throughout this room.

Tobe noticed a scent, one that he'd always enjoyed. It smelled like a library in here. The aroma of old, printed pages was a smell that had always elated him, even as a child. It made sense this room would smell like that with all the old posters and paper everywhere.

At the doorway, Tobe glanced back at Gearhart from over his shoulder.

"Go on," he said, giving him permission to enter without him.

Tobe nodded. It felt as if his mouth might have smiled an appreciation, but he couldn't tell. Everything felt so odd that he wondered if he was even awake. Maybe he'd fallen down the stairs and broken his neck or had passed out at the front door when he realized the homeowner was the *real* John Gearhart, and this was some kind of unconscious fantasy.

Tobe stepped through the doorway, into a room that was even dimmer than the theater. There were bookcases spanning from one wall to the other on either side. Books filled some of the shelves, and the others were occupied with a back stock of even more memorabilia. His eyes scanned masks, fake hands, some latex puppets. Creatures (or pieces of them) from Gearhart's films. There were original shooting scripts, more lobby cards, and even some old-fashioned model kits from the fifties that were probably worth a lot of money.

It was like being in a museum full of artifacts that only Tobe cared about. His heart was rapping against his chest with such force he could feel it in his throat. He felt dizzy, but not like he was going to faint. This was the kind of dizziness that came with excitement, the same kind he used to get on Christmas morning while peeping at presents Santa had left under the tree before his parents had wakened.

He spent a few more minutes in here, admiring the collectibles before finally forcing himself to leave. John Gearhart was waiting for him in a theater seat, his legs crossed casually as he gave Tobe time to finish exploring.

When he saw Tobe exiting the room, he smiled. "A lot of junk, huh?"

"*Amazing* junk."

"I kept everything."

"I can tell. It's…awesome."

"Thanks. You know, I owned my own independent studio. We had an office in Macon, and there was even more stuff in our storage shed that disappeared over the years. So I'm sure there's stuff of mine floating around out there that I don't remember ever having, but I think what I've managed to salvage is plenty."

"It's great."

"Thank you. I thought you might get a kick out of it." He stood up. There was something in his hand. "Here." He offered it to Tobe. "You might like this."

"Wha…?" Tobe walked over to him and took the object. It was the script from his first movie, the one that was probably his most influential. *A Georgia Battle-axe Massacre.* And it looked to have been signed by everyone involved with the making of the movie. The pages had yellowed with age and temperature damage, but the font was legible. The copyright date down in the left corner was 1969.

"Wow…" Tobe's throat tightened. "I couldn't…"

"Please, take it. You obviously love this stuff as much as I do."

"Th-thank you."

"You're welcome."

He felt as if he might cry. Taking a deep breath, he hoped to find his bearings again. "Want to go on and do the paperwork?"

"Sure. If you don't have anywhere to be right after, I was going to make some sandwiches for dinner. I can make you one as well. And we can talk about movies."

"Wow, thank you so much. I don't want to be a bother…"

"Hardly. We don't get much company out here. Especially ones with a love for movies like me."

Tobe smiled. "Okay. I will. So long as you're sure you don't mind."

"I don't mind."

How amazing is this? Getting to eat dinner with John Gearhart!

His wife would never believe this. Thankfully he had the script to show her as proof. He felt like calling his best friend from years ago and telling him about it—*brag* about it! They hadn't spoken in a couple years, but for over a decade they were inseparable, and shared the same affection for horror.

Back in the hallway, Tobe waited as Gearhart closed the door to the basement.

"Thank you, again, for showing me all of that."

Gearhart nodded. "My pleasure." They began to walk back to the dining room. "Do I need to bring anything to this signing? It's been so long since I've refinanced, I can't remember what all I need to bring to the table."

"Just your ID so I can jot down the information. I know who you are, so I'm not using it for verification." He laughed softly. "Is your wife a co-borrower?"

"No. Is that a problem?"

"No, it shouldn't be, but since this is a spousal state, there might be some documents she needs to sign."

He nodded. "Want me to go get her?"

"If you want to. There might not be anything she needs to sign, but you never know."

"I'll go fetch her." He smiled. "Just in case."

"Okay. Sounds good."

"She'll get a kick out of you. I can't wait to introduce you."

"I can't wait to meet her."

"Be right back."

Gearhart left Tobe alone in the dining room. He heard Gearhart call out, "Honey?" That was followed by the swish of his feet on the stairs as he went up.

Tobe sat down on the right-hand side of the table, deciding against the head seat. He figured it would be easier if John sat there, with his wife Glenda across from Tobe. That way the documents could be passed in a circle instead of back and forth, which would make the whole process smoother.

Tobe was nervous about meeting Mrs. Gearhart. He knew the story of how they'd met on the set of *A Georgia Battle-axe Massacre* and that they'd been together ever since. He'd read about her so much in Gearhart's books and interviews that he felt like he knew her already. He'd never seen any pictures of her, though. He wondered if she was an actress, a make-up lady, or one of the crew members. What would she look like now? Would he recognize her?

He flipped through the typed script while he waited. It was held together by clasps in the three-ring holes. The print's fading was noticeable, but he still smiled, knowing it had been penned on a typewriter. Tobe had used one when he was a teenager to write his own horror movies. It had been so much fun, and he missed it. The excitement he had while doing it, the smell of the ink being hammered into the paper, and the steady chorus of clacking that had engulfed his room while he'd write. He had spent much of his free time hunched over that old machine as a teenager.

He sat the script down, leaned over, and opened his briefcase on the floor. He removed his notary stamp and the two sets of documents. They were ninety pages each—one for Gearhart to sign that Tobe had to send back and the other stack was for him to leave here. He sat them on the table, sliding Gearhart's copies off to the side. Removing the cap from his stamp, he pushed the button, and extended it. He placed it at his right hand. Then he dropped the script in the briefcase. He didn't want to risk leaving it behind when he left.

The house was uncomfortably quiet. He couldn't hear the sounds of nature from outside. From somewhere in the house came the ticking of a clock. Then there was a thump from upstairs, followed by some footsteps.

A door bumped.

Gearhart was talking quietly. It sounded as if he was answering a question, though Tobe couldn't hear what had been asked.

The squeaking clomps on the stairs resonated again. It sounded like there was only one set of feet.

Who was he talking to?

When Gearhart entered the room, Tobe nearly shrieked at what he saw.

"Tobe. This is Glenda, my wife."

What was *this*? A joke? There was no way Gearhart was serious. Was he putting him on?

As much as Tobe hoped so, he could tell by the proud smile on the man's face, and the pure delight in his eyes that he was *not* joking. This *thing* he cradled in his arms was his wife.

And Tobe *did* recognize her.

Her face had been constructed out of clay, and from the brittle dryness of it, decades ago. There were cracks running through the foundation and one eye was missing, a hollow orifice. The other eye was a plastic ball, with a painted cornea in the middle that had probably once been blue, but had since faded to a dull gray.

Blonde hair was stapled to the forehead of the artificial head. He could see the rusted lines of the staples clamped in the hairline. The hair itself was dry and clumped, mussed in patches and stringy in others. There was a large fake nose, chipped on the tip, that Tobe swore was probably taken from a Groucho Marx glasses, nose, and moustache kit. And her lips were thick pulpy wax that looked like the same packaged brand Tobe would get in his trick-or-treat bag at Halloween. They were pulled back into a bogus grimace, revealing jagged false teeth for a mouth.

There was even less care in the craftsmanship of the body. Its skeletal arms and legs were the girth of corn stalks, and the torso was flat with two nubs for breasts. The skin looked like decaying rubber and was just as ashy-toned as the face. A flimsy nightie draped the middle of her thighs and when Gearhart lifted her into the chair across from Tobe, he was able to glance between her legs. He felt sick when he saw the tight, flaky ingress and sculpted vulva around it. A patch of dingy coiled hair that matched the color of the wig had been glued above it.

Tobe had guessed correctly that Gearhart had married one of the stars of his movies. And yes, she had starred in his first movie, but she wasn't one of the actresses. She was a prop—a dead body prop that was discovered in the killer's bedroom by a hapless victim.

Oh shit, oh shit. This is crazy, this is so fucking crazy.

Any moment he expected, *hoped*, Gearhart would start laughing and jab a finger in his ribs, saying he'd gotten him. Then he'd bring his *real* wife into the room and introduce *her* instead.

As much as Tobe would have appreciated that, he knew it wasn't going to happen.

This was Gearhart's wife.

"Glenda, this is Tobe. He's the one I was telling you about." He lifted her arm. It popped and cracked as it shifted on its chicken-wire torso. The extended hand was a glob of painted latex. Wired fingers were exposed in patches where the foam had deteriorated.

Tobe only stared, at a loss as to what he should do. He glanced at Gearhart and saw the man's smile slightly falter. Then he realized he was supposed to shake her hand. He reached up and was surprised to see his hand wasn't trembling as bad as his hips and legs were. Gearhart's smile returned in full force. Tobe took her hand in his. It felt like dried paper mache, and sticky like old bubble gum.

"Now, now, be a gentleman Tobe and kiss her hand."

Tobe's stomach gurgled. He felt as if at any moment he was going to vomit the beef jerky he'd eaten on the drive out here all over this mock woman's chest. He tried to think of a hundred reasons he could tell Gearhart that he had to leave, but his mind was like a blank sheet of paper. Unable to come up with anything, he finally leaned forward and put his lips to the crackly dry flesh.

It tasted awful, like tires that would be on the bottom of a car in a junkyard. He felt acid at the back of his throat and swallowed several times, hoping to keep it there.

"Atta boy!" Smiling, Gearhart ambled around the back of Glenda's chair to sit at the one Tobe had preselected for him. "I guess we should get started. I don't know about you, but I'm about ready to eat."

Tobe had completely forgotten about the sandwiches they were supposed to enjoy later. Funny how he'd been eager to share a meal with John Gearhart and now he was dreading it. What was he going to do? How was he going to be able to leave without making it obvious he didn't want to be here?

"So what color do we use?" asked Gearhart.

"Huh?" Tobe tore his eyes away from the disgusting form of Glenda. "What?"

"I know she's pretty…but don't gawk at her right in front of me." He winked, nudging at Tobe with an elbow.

Tobe *was* staring. He shook his head, hoping to jar the fuzz in his brain free. Then he reached into his briefcase on the floor and fetched two pens. "Blue…" His voice came out croaky, so he cleared his throat and repeated himself.

"Blue?" asked Gearhart. "That's odd."

"They all want blue ink these days. It's harder to counterfeit in scans and copies."

"Ah. That makes sense."

Tobe took a deep breath and pinched his eyes shut for a moment, then exhaled slowly. "Let's get started."

John Gearhart took his time reading over the documents. This aggravated Tobe even when he wasn't trapped in a room with a synthetically made woman and a palpable whacko. He understood the borrowers needed to know what they were signing, but it amazed him they never asked the lenders any of their questions beforehand. Plus, they had three days to read over the documents and have any changes they deemed necessary made.

Tobe tried to pretend Glenda wasn't sitting across from him, staring at him with that one, faded plastic eye.

She's not real, he reminded himself.

It didn't matter. In some strange way, it seemed even worse knowing that she wasn't.

Thankfully Gearhart didn't ask any questions about the loan, because Tobe doubted he had the voice to respond. But he read every word of the ninety-page packet. In between pages, he would stop signing long enough to tell Tobe a story about one of his films, either something from the making of it or some useless fact about its release. This would have amused Tobe, under regular circumstances.

These were hardly *regular* circumstances!

Tobe was stuck here. He was following the signing company's motto and didn't want to disappoint them. Regardless of the situation, he was being paid to stay professional and courteous, with a smile on his face and a devoted awareness at all times.

Besides, he would have felt lousy running out on the old director, especially after he'd given him the movie script. So he offered up a hefty dose of bullshit laughter at the appropriate times, nodded his head to replicate interest and concern. But whenever Gearhart smiled his amiable smile, it nearly brought Tobe to tears, because he knew the truth really was that he was observing the actions of a very lonely and delusional old man.

He remembered being a kid when his grandmother passed away, and the uncomfortable visits with his grandfather afterward. His Grandpa used to be a voluble man, always telling jokes in a boomingly loud voice. But after Grandma's death, he became a withering man in a recliner, never talking, only grunting and nodding his head whenever spoken to—a man waiting to die. Tobe had been too young to understand then, but as an adult, it was easy to see.

Gearhart was finishing up the last page. Usually, it would be time for Tobe to produce his notary log for the borrower to fill out, that way he had a record of the signing for tax purposes. He was going to skip it this time. He was ready to vamoose, though he still hadn't thought of a way out.

Text Kaylyn, he suddenly thought, *and tell her to call me and pretend there's an emergency.*

He quickly fumbled his phone out of his pocket and pulled up the dial screen. The top three names were his emergency contacts. Kaylyn was at the top. He quickly selected her name and began fingering a message.

Call me. Pretnd there s emergency. I explain lates.

He quickly read it. Even with poor grammar, she should get the essence of it.

Send.

He looked up, finding Gearhart's eyes locked on him. Their accusatory gleam was magnified behind the thick lenses of his glasses. There was no way he could have known what he was texting. Tobe had kept his hands below the table.

Then Tobe realized what the deal was. He would bet it was his guilty-looking face. Whenever he was trying to hide something, his bottom lip seemed to want to hide under the top one and he would suddenly forget how to blink. He purposely made himself blink a few times just to show Gearhart nothing was wrong.

"What's wrong?" he asked.

Damn.

Tobe shook his head. "Nothing. Why?"

"You look like something's wrong."

Here's my chance.

"Oh, well…my wife texted me a few minutes ago saying there's something going on with her aunt and well…she might have to leave, so I need to get home as soon as possible to be with the kids. I'm waiting on her to call."

"Oh no!"

"Yeah." He nodded, puckering his lip as if he was heartbroken. Kaylyn's aunt lived in Oklahoma and was fine, so far as Tobe knew, but Gearhart didn't need to know that. He hated lying about having sick relatives, but felt it was justifiable this once.

"Well, I'll get started on those sandwiches. If you have to leave you can take some with you."

Tobe collapsed back into the chair, like a balloon deflating. Gearhart had bought the lie.

"I have hoagie bread and deli-sliced ham, turkey, and even roast beef. I'm not a big fan of salami, but there is some bologna in there, if you want it. What would you like?"

It all sounded good. He could feel his hunger returning. If he didn't accept the offer for a sandwich, not only would he hurt Gearhart's feelings, he'd have to stop at a drive-thru or gas station on his way home. He didn't want the heartburn later and he also didn't want to spend the money.

So what if Gearhart's *wife* had been created with chicken wire, derma wax, and latex? He could ignore it for a free meal, right? He could focus his attention on the sandwich and pretend he'd never been introduced to Glenda, right?

Nope!

Kaylyn better hurry up and call.

"A ham and turkey sandwich sounds good…" His voice moistened with acidic spittle near the end.

Gearhart smiled. "Want anything on it? I love sandwiches so I make sure I have all the elements to make them on hand. Lettuce? Tomato?"

"Yeah…that would be good. Both, please."

"Mustard?"

Tobe nodded. "Sounds good."

Laughing, Gearhart clapped his hands together like a mastermind whose plan had been unleashed. The loud slap made Tobe flinch.

Gearhart stood up. "I'll get started."

"I'll come with you."

"No, no. Stay here and keep Glenda company. She *hates* being left alone for extended periods of time, just downright despises it. I'll be a little while assembling the meat and cutting the veggies. Get acquainted."

Tobe lost his appetite again. He wondered if he looked as pale and sickly as he felt. An image of Gearhart returning with two plates of plastic hoagies popped into his head. He wouldn't be surprised at this point.

Gearhart patted the back of the chair he'd been occupying. "Take my seat. She doesn't hear quite as well as she used to."

No, Mr. Gearhart. She doesn't hear at all! *She's not real. She's something put together by an FX man, a long time ago!*

Standing up, Tobe felt his shirt clinging to his back and sides from the gelid sweat trickling down him. He checked his shirt to make sure there weren't any visible sweat stains. There weren't. It was cool in the house, but Tobe couldn't stop sweating as if he was outside in the damp heat.

Gearhart pulled the chair out as if he was on a date. Tobe started to sit as the chair was scooted under his butt. He dropped into it, weak and famished.

"Have fun, you two." He leaned down, his mouth close to Tobe's ear. "Don't you try anything funny." There was sincere threat in his voice.

"Don't worry," he gulped. "I won't…"

"I trust you."

Gearhart squeezed Tobe's shoulder. He left the room, and Tobe was alone with Glenda. He could smell the fetid odor of mildew, mold, and old clay. The stink reminded him of his grandma's purse. She would keep makeup in the bag for years, way past its point of expiration, so even the gum she regularly carried around tasted like it. He looked at Glenda. Her plastic eye seemed to gaze straight through him to the wall behind him. He shivered. He had to find something to do, something to occupy his time.

Get the package ready for shipping?

That works.

Turning his back to her, he gathered up the papers, arranged them into a neat stack, and slid them into a Fed-Ex envelope bag. He sealed it. Finished, he dropped it in the case, closing the lid.

Checking his phone, he saw that Kaylyn hadn't called or texted him back. What was taking her so long? She'd probably put her phone on the counter and left it there. Chances were, she hadn't even noticed he'd texted.

Should he call her, tell her to call him right back?

Gearhart might hear him.

He glanced over his shoulder, saw Glenda still gaping at him with that craggy, crooked grin, and quickly got out of his chair. He needed to move around. Sitting seemed to make it worse. He stretched his taut muscles, his lower back and legs. His body felt sore, like it would after a long drive.

Tobe decided to walk around the room. Maybe if he kept moving it would help ease his tension. As he paced around the table, he stole peeks of Glenda from the corner of his eye. Her gaze seemed to never leave him, like one of those old paintings that watched you no matter where you went in the room.

As he walked to the other end of the dining table, he spotted the small writing table nestled in the corner of the room. He vaguely remembered seeing it when he'd first entered the room. Being this close, he saw that sitting on top was a photo album with white candle sticks on either side.

His curiosity carried him even closer to the table. The book was blue and string bound. In gold, ornamental lettering on the front was *Cherished Memories.*

He wanted to look inside.

Checking that Gearhart wasn't about to enter the room, and making sure Glenda wasn't watching him, he opened the album. On the first page was a black-and-white 8 x 10 photo of Glenda in better health. She looked as if she'd just come from the make-up artist's workshop. Her hair looked lively and as vibrant as could be expected from a cheap wig.

Tobe turned the page to another black-and-white of a much younger Gearhart. Where he was now white-haired was black curls, and his face was free of any stress lines and wrinkles. He was kneeling beside Glenda as she lay on the bed in a scene from *A Georgia Battle-axe Massacre*. Tobe recognized even in the still that Gearhart was being flirty with her. With a prop! And someone had documented this?

He skipped a few pages ahead. This one looked to be in a restaurant. There were others in the background, watching with proud smiles on their faces as Glenda was seated at her own table with a half-eaten plate of food and an empty wine glass in front of her. The real kicker was Gearhart—down on one knee, his hands in an offering position. Resting on his palm was an opened ring case with a blocky, diamond ring snuggled inside.

"You've got to be kidding me," he muttered.

The proposal. And somebody had documented this as well. Tobe tried to imagine the kind of person who'd sit by and snap photographs of a man's mental collapse instead of finding him psychological help.

He pinched a chunk of pages and turned them, landing on the big kiss at the wedding ceremony. Glenda was dressed in white with a vale draped over the back of her head like a curtain. She was standing to the left, and Gearhart was on the right, a hand on each side of her face, his thin lips pressed to her fat, waxed ones. A priest stood abreast of them, smiling, and Tobe noticed a single tear streaming from the man of God's right eye.

Someone had actually performed a ceremony. Were there people in attendance? Did they applaud and cheer after the kiss was over?

"Jesus," he mumbled.

He closed the book. There was a lump in his throat that he couldn't swallow, and his back felt as if he'd had acupuncture performed on him with icicles.

I've got to get out of here. Forget waiting for Kaylyn to call. She probably won't even notice the text until it's too late.

Too late? What did he really think was going to happen to him here?

A man who'd been married to a dead-body prop for more than forty years was capable of about anything. And he'd already accused Tobe of being overly cute with Glenda. What would happen if there was another allegation?

Tobe didn't want to know.

He turned around. Glenda hadn't moved. He'd almost expected her to be standing up, a knife clutched in her decomposing, wire-made hand. She was in the same spot, as she should be.

Crossing the room, Tobe snatched his briefcase up in one quick swoop, and was standing at the doorway in less than two seconds. His breaths were arduous wheezes, and he could feel sweat on his brow, gluing his hair to his forehead. His mouth had gone dry and tasted coppery.

He leaned his head out, turning left and then right. He saw the kitchen was across the hall, just under the staircase. He could hear movement in there, some clattering around. He couldn't see Gearhart. However, he could see the lip of an island, pots and pans dangling from hooks above it. On the other side was the counter, and from where he stood he spotted a section of a stainless-steal sink.

Tobe didn't wait for Gearhart to appear. His feet were moving his body into the hallway and towards the front door before his mind had given the order to do so. Luckily Gearhart had left the main door open, and all that separated Tobe from being outside was the screen door.

The length of the hallway seemed to be stretching, moving the door farther away from him. Tobe knew it actually wasn't, but damn it, what was taking him so long to reach the exit?

Finally, it was near enough to touch.

He reached for it.

And his cell phone's ringtone erupted in the silent stretch, sounding like a mass of metal being dropped in an aluminum room.

Of course, he'd forgotten to turn off his ringer. Of course, he'd chosen the old rotary sound for his ringer, which was the loudest of them all. And of course, Kaylyn would pick *now* to call! He knew without looking that the display screen would show *The Wife* as being the caller.

He looked over his shoulder. Gearhart stepped halfway into the hall. The other part of his body was hidden behind the doorway. Grasped in his left hand was a butcher knife. "Where are you going?" he shouted. Gone was his polite tenor. Gone was his smile, his friendly eyes. What occupied his face now was an angry scowl.

"Oh sorry," Tobe said. "But I have to go!"

Gearhart shook his head. "No! You're staying for dinner!" He wasn't saying this like a man attempting to persuade someone into staying longer. It was an order. "You will *not* leave!"

"Fuck you, man. I'm going!" Tobe shoved the screen door open, giving one more look over his shoulder. Gearhart was charging towards him, and moving faster than Tobe expected him to be. "Shit!"

The muggy air slithered over him as he raced across the porch and down the steps. He lost his footing when his shoes hit the gravel of the driveway, but he managed to stay up. For a flare of a second, he'd forgotten where he'd parked. There was only one place he could have and that was *in* the driveway, which was located directly ahead of him.

And there sat his Jeep, waiting for him like a kind friend. His phone continued to clamor from his pocket. He didn't want to stop long enough to answer it.

The door busted open behind him. "Stop!"

Oh shit oh shit…he's coming!

"I trusted you! Glenda liked you!"

"Glenda's *not real*," Tobe shouted without looking back.

"How could you say such a thing?"

Tobe's side banged against the Jeep, he said, "Because it's the truth," then twirled around to the driver's side, his hands fumbling with the door handle. He yanked it open. Thankfully, he'd forgotten to lock it.

He didn't forget, though, once he was inside.

The staccato sound of four doors and a rear gate locking was glorious. Through the windshield he could see Gearhart had slowed his pace. He was hardly running now, not even trotting, more like a brisk walk. The waning light glinted off the knife's blade.

Tobe fished his keys out from his left pocket, then his phone from the right. When he shoved the key into the ignition, he noticed Gearhart had turned his back on him and was returning to the porch.

What's he doing?

He kept his eyes aimed at Gearhart while he cranked the car. Air blew from the vents. Warm at first, it quickly cooled. He cranked the dial back up to high.

Gearhart watched him from the porch, a shadowy shape under the eave. He had his hands on his hips, the blade of the knife angled away from his body like a gleaming barb. He no longer looked mad.

He was frowning.

Ashamed? Embarrassed?

Possibly.

Most likely, he was just sad.

Tobe felt crummy. He hadn't done anything wrong. He'd acted how anyone else given the same situation would have. He might have even saved his own life. So why did he feel like he'd stolen stacks of money from Gearhart's hidden safe?

Putting the car into reverse, he backed around a light post, and turned the wheel sharply to the left. He shifted to drive and sped away, throwing up gravel behind his tires.

He stared in the rearview mirror. Gearhart became smaller and smaller until eventually the sagging tree limbs filled the glass completely and he could no longer see him.

Once he was at the mouth of Windy Circle where it met the paved road, his phone rang again. This time, he dug it from his pocket and answered.

"What's going on?" asked Kaylyn without a greeting.

"I'll tell you later."

"Is everything okay?"

"Yeah...I suppose..." He sighed. "I don't know."

"You sound awful. What happened?"

"I can't talk about it right now...I just want to get home."

"Was it the John Gearhart you wanted it to be?"

Tobe sighed. "Yeah..."

"What happened? Was he an asshole?"

He laughed, though it lacked humor. "No. Actually, he was..."

"What?"

Sighing, he said, "He wasn't what I thought he would be."

"I'm sorry."

"It's okay. I'll give you all the details when I get home."

They said their *I love yous* and hung up.

As Tobe drove the scenic route back, he decided that once he reached civilization again, he would find a gas station and pull in.

He needed cigarettes.

Story Notes:

I'm sure it's no surprise that I love horror movies. The passion began when I was five years old and saw *Friday the 13th* for the first time, way back in 1984. My love for the genre spans a wide range, though I find it difficult to enjoy a lot of the newer films that aren't sequels to the classics. Maybe it's my stubbornness, but I don't think anything can beat the old stuff. The list of horror filmmakers that I adore is quite long and John Gearhart is a hodgepodge of them all.

A lot of writers, myself included, usually can't say where an idea for a story comes from. Most of the time, they just pop in my head. One minute I'm thinking about food and the next thing I know something knocks that thought out of the way and a story has hatched. Not with *Gearhart's Wife.* I know exactly where this idea came from: It was my job as a Notary Signing Agent.

My duties included taking mortgage paperwork to the borrowers' homes to sign and notarize and I was responsible for shipping them back to the lenders. One day, I received an order for a borrower with the name John Carpenter. Sure, that's quite the common name, but the entire drive over there, I kept fantasizing about the borrower being the *real* John Carpenter who opens the door. I pictured him smoking a cigarette, wearing all black, while the soundtrack to *Escape From New York* blared from a stereo somewhere inside. To my disappointment, it wasn't the same John Carpenter. On the drive home, the story formed itself in my head and I wrote it that night.

Even now, all these years later, it's still one of my favorites.

A fun fact that I've never shared until now is that John Gearhart was actually in the original draft of my novel, *Proud Parents.* There's a scene where the characters go to a horror convention because one of them is a guest and he invites his neighbors to sit with him at his table. Greg Heyman, the neighbor, sneaks outside to have a cigarette and bumps into John Gearhart, who's enjoying a cigarette. Turns out he's a guest there as well and they have a small exchange.

I loved the scene, but in the end, I felt it only slowed down the third act when the momentum was switching to rapid-fire. Still, I hated to see it go.

But, to have a little fun, here's the scene, unedited:

Dim lighting made it difficult to see, but the red glow of an exit sign guided Greg in the right direction. He arrived at the door, found the bar, and pushed it down. It sprung open, throwing bright warmth onto him. He squinted so hard his eyes watered. The heat was heavy on his clothes as he stepped outside.

"Catch the door!" he heard a man shout.

Greg caught the door by the handle just before it closed. "Got it!"

"Thank God," the man said. "I've been locked out here for ten minutes. Times like these make me wish I owned a cell phone. Could've just called someone to come let me in."

Greg nearly gasped when he realized who the voice belonged to. John Gearhart, a popular horror director who'd directed a slew of films that Greg had grown up watching. *A Georgia Massacre* was one of Greg's favorites of all time. Sheila would never believe this.

"Door locks when it shuts, I take it?" asked Greg.

"You bet. Come out for a smoke and you're left to bake. This heat is something, huh?"

"Yeah. Summer's definitely here."

"It's okay. My favorite time of the year anyway."

"I like it, too."

John squinted his eyes, regarding Greg curiously. "Do I know you?"

Greg felt a slight flutter of concern. "I don't know. Do you?"

"Maybe you have one of those faces."

Smiling, Greg shrugged. "I get that."

"I bet so."

"I know who *you* are, though."

"Yeah?"

Greg nodded. "John freakin' Gearhart!"

The old man laughed, nodding. His snow-colored mustached curved upward with his smile. "That's me." The hair on his head was wavy and gray, the bangs clung against his forehead from sweat.

"I didn't know you were a guest here this weekend."

Gearhart shrugged. "Don't know if you can consider me a guest."

"Why do say that?" Greg kicked down the stand on the door to hold it open.

"Well," said Gearhart, "they've got me tossed in the backroom with the dealers. All those people from that zombie show got all the good spots."

Greg frowned. "That sucks."

"I'll live. What sucks is I want another cigarette and left mine in my bag at my table."

"I'll give you one."

"You're a kind soul."

Laughing, Greg walked over to the knee-high ash tray. Sand had been dumped into the basin. Crinkled butts jutted like twisted little worms. Greg held out the opened pack. The old man pinched a filter and slid one out.

After the cigarettes were lighted, Gearhart turned to Greg. "So are you a guest? A fan?"

"Neither. Well...I suppose I could be considered a fan, but that's not why I'm here."

Gearhart's eyes narrowed. "I don't follow."

"Well..." Greg didn't know how much he should say, but he figured it was safe to share a little bit of it with Gearhart. "You know Todd Parker?"

"The author?"

"That's him. He's my neighbor and, well...I'm a comic book artist looking for work, so Todd thought..."

"If you tagged along, he could introduce you to some people?"

"Yeah...in a sense."

"That's a good friend. I'll tell you, in this business, no one likes to stick their necks out for each other because usually, it gets broken."

"The neck?"

"Oh yeah. Sometimes, in multiple places."

"Ouch."

"Yeah...it's nothing that I'm proud of, but it happens."

"You get your neck broken?"

Gearhart patted the front of his throat. "Yes. So many times, I'm surprised I don't have to constantly wear a brace."

"I'm sorry to hear that."

"Nature of the beast, I suppose. But if your neighbor is willing to vouch for you, in this day and age, then you must be good people."

Suddenly Greg felt like he was suffocating. His mouth went dry, and the cigarette smoke was like powdered chalk on his tongue. Gearhart's words struck him in the chest like a sideways hand chop. Greg didn't feel as if he was much of a good person. He'd done too many things he wasn't proud of. He'd hurt a lot of people. But Todd was a genuinely good guy, the first benevolent person Greg had come across in a very long time.

"He's not a homo is he?" asked Gearhart.

The blunt question evaporated the fog in Greg's head. "What?"

"I see the wedding ring on your hand, so I don't suppose *you* are.But if he's a homo, he might be promising you things just to get at your tally-whacker."

Greg huffed out a cloud of smoke as he sighed. He tried reminding himself Gearhart was from a different time and probably didn't realize how small-minded he sounded. It didn't work. "It was nice meeting you, Mr. Gearhart." Greg stuffed the cigarette into the sand.

THE NIGHT EVERYTHING CHANGED

*T*he wind was picking up. All week the weathermen warned of severe thunderstorms making their way into the heart of Wisconsin, but, until recently, the weather had been chipper. These early days of June had been almost perfect.

Lightning flashed with a boom of thunder. Rain would come soon, probably within minutes. The lingering odor of manure that usually fortified the farmlands had all but been dispersed by the wind.

Dr. Vincent Carlson darted from his house. He'd forgotten to latch the front barn door and heard it pounding against the side of the stable. The last thing he needed was to trot all over the land during a storm and gather up escaped animals. If it were any other night, he'd get his daughter, Leanne, to help round them up, but she'd been at the carnival all evening and wasn't here to help if the stock got out.

Vincent had implored her not to go, but she'd insisted. He didn't like the idea of her running off to some strange carnival where the main attraction was a herd of tiny people, even if it was on his land. Not dwarves, mind you, these *people* were even smaller.

He'd heard rumblings in town that some folks thought they might be elves.

That was ridiculous. Elves.

Leanne argued it was the eighties, times had changed, and people could believe what they wanted and go to any kind of carnival that they wanted without worry of being ridiculed for it.

Vincent wasn't the only one in Doverton who wasn't thrilled that the Haunchies had rolled into town.

He was sure Leanne would have plenty to say about what the other townspeople were thinking. She was a teenager and had just graduated from South Doverton High School. Of course, she knew everything. Her brain was a mass of uncultivated knowledge.

She was a very smart girl, preparing this summer to start college near Green Bay in the fall. And Vincent wasn't scared to admit to anyone he'd miss her terribly.

He grabbed the barn door just as the wind gusted it open, catching it before it smacked against the side wall. Keeping it gripped firmly with both hands, he inspected the door as the wind wobbled it like sheet metal. It was a strain to keep a firm hold on it. He saw the door was already showing evidence of damage. The wood was old, but he'd hoped it would last at least a couple more years. After this abuse, he'd probably have to repair it by the Fourth of July.

Using both hands, he pushed the door against the blustery weather, and, after a bit of a struggle, managed to slam it shut. He dropped the latch in place, securing the door closed and pulled on the plank, checking its durability. It felt sturdy enough. He hoped it would hold.

Another twisting bolt of lightning crackled down from the sky, striking a tree somewhere deep in the woods, across from Vincent's cornfields. The explosion made him jump out of his skin.

Storm's getting closer.

He hugged himself. What little heat they'd had during this early part of the summer was gone. In Wisconsin, the summers normally felt like fall, and when fall did come, it was nearly as cold as the winter. The weather never matched the season.

"Leanne better be getting on home," he muttered.

Why hadn't she gotten home yet? He'd told her no later than midnight. It had been steadily approaching that time when he'd last checked the clock in the house. It was probably midnight by now, but if not, it was damn close.

As Vincent hurried back to the house, he recalled the flyer Leanne had shown him. It was an advertisement for the carnival, one of the many he'd already seen stapled to the power poles in town and taped across the windows and walls of any buildings whose owners had granted them permission.

Written in flashy letters was:

The Final Tour of the Haunchyville Carnival!
Come enjoy it while you still can!

He shouldn't have let her talk him into it.

When she'd brought him the flyer, she wasn't just showing him that they were coming. She'd been using it to help explain why Vincent should offer them his fields for their last run in the Midwest. They'd lost their original location at the fairgrounds in Bixby and traveled south, trying to find another place to stake their tents.

Like a fool, Vincent had obliged.

Haunchyville. Such an awful name. Why those little people had selected that name for their traveling group was beyond him. Maybe for the little ones it was okay. He couldn't fairly vouch for their way of thinking. After all, he was only the town doctor, so what he figured probably didn't count for much.

But he hated the name all the same.

Leanne sure knew a lot about the group. He was taken aback by how much knowledge she had. It was a little unnerving. She'd sat Vincent down at the kitchen table the same night she'd shown him the flyer and explained what she knew of the carnival's history, explained that they weren't really dwarves at all. She told him more about the Haunchies than any rational person needed to know.

Even though he hadn't wanted to hear any of it, he'd sat and listened. She was good at that, getting him to give in to anything she wanted. Probably because she had her mother's eyes, brightly blue as the sky and round as tires.

Leanne was the spitting image of her as well. Another reason why Vincent wished she'd stayed home instead of lollygagging around the carnival. He didn't care if it was his land they had set up on, he still didn't relish the idea of her being there. She would be the best-looking gal there. Most of the women and even teenage girls of Doverton were his patients, and, sure, some of them were cute, pretty even, but none could hold a candle to Leanne.

She was as beautiful as the girls in magazines. Her beauty made him proud, yet at the same time, made his chest heavy with concern. Sometimes, he'd get so worked up fretting over her he feared he might have a heart attack.

Vincent stepped under the eave of his front porch just as the rain began plummeting in heavy drops. He decided to wait here on the porch until he saw the headlights of his truck coming around the bend in the cornfield. A dirt road segmented the fields and Leanne had chosen to call it Mystic Lane. Vincent, always the encouraging father, even had a sign made with the name chiseled into it. They'd taken it into the fields and hammered it into the ground just like any other road sign you'd see. He'd never forgotten how happy it had made her.

He was thankful that, out of his fear of the weather turning bad, he'd talked her into taking the truck. Once he spotted the headlights peering through the stalks, he'd go inside. Lord knew he wouldn't dare let Leanne catch him waiting for her.

She hated that.

But with the way the rain was slashing down from the sky like sideways wet daggers, he doubted he'd be able to see much at all beyond the front yard. The fields were like black blobs in the storm. Vincent could only see the corn in the burst of a lightning flash.

In the morning, he'd surely find batches of stalks had been blown over, and he'd lose money because of it. Why did he keep putting himself through the hassle and expense of maintaining them? Being the town doctor made him more than enough money, but for whatever reason, he'd chosen to take on the duties of the family farm as well.

Ma and Pa Carlson had both passed away in the winter of '81. A freak hay-baling accident had taken both of their lives. Vincent had just buried his lovely wife and the mother of his child a few months before. They were living in Appleton at the time, but once Margaret passed, Vincent had no desire to stay in that house or that town any longer.

It had been written in his parents' will that the Carlson farm, house, and the acres of land surrounding it were to be left to Vincent. He gladly turned in his notice at the hospital, packed up their belongings, and moved with Leanne to Doverton.

And for the past six years he and Leanne had been handling the farm on their own. It'd been tough at times, but they'd made it through all right. However, with her leaving for school in the fall, he would have to hire on some help if he was going to keep the farm going. There was no way he could preserve the nineteen acres of crops himself. That didn't include the surrounding two hundred acres of woodland, plus the other fifty acres of fields. The house was already greatly isolated from the rest of Doverton in the nearly three hundred acres his family owned. It was as if the rest of the world was nonexistent.

He didn't mind living on the farm. He'd grown up on the land, and it was nice raising his daughter in such a small town. He could keep an eye on her, making sure she stayed out of trouble. Or so he hoped. Leanne would have all this land to herself one day, and the three-story farmhouse with it. She'd be more than taken care of once he'd gone to his own greener pastures.

"All right, now. Enough is enough. Time to get home, girl." Even speaking only to himself, his voice sounded worried.

He paced the front porch for several more minutes, then headed inside to check the time. Standing in the living room, he glanced at the grandfather clock by the fireplace.

12:31.

A shot of dread hit Vincent in the chest. Something was wrong. He knew it. Leanne had never been late, ever. If she knew she was going to be, she would have called him. But there had been no phone call, so that meant she wasn't expecting to be late, which could only mean...

Something had happened.

But what?

Vincent didn't know, but he planned to find out. First, he needed to come up with a plan. Actions couldn't be taken without the proper preparation.

He sat in his favorite chair, an old, cushioned rocker, to think. As he glided back and forth, he combed his thoughts for a game plan.

He was certain the carnival was over by now. He'd have to take the tractor since Leanne had the truck, and it would probably take him twenty to thirty minutes to get to the pasture gate on Mystic Lane.

What if they've locked it?

That was simple. He'd break the damn lock. After all, it was *his* gate, and *his* property they were squatting on.

Why did he need a plan? He should just ride out there and, if he needed to, drag Leanne kicking and screaming back home. It'd serve her right for being so late.

Absorbed by his thoughts, Vincent nearly missed the pitter-patter of little feet darting across his front porch. It sounded like the footsteps of children playing tag on the stoop.

It made his skin crawl.

He stood up. The rocking chair knocked against the backs of his legs. He crept to the double-bay windows that looked out on the porch. He'd have a nice view of the porch and even a partial look at the yard. He could see his own reflection in the glass. It looked as if there were two of him, both slinking to meet at the window. The brightness inside made it impossible to see into the darkness outside.

Vincent pressed his face to the glass as if he and his reflection were trying to clumsily kiss. He placed his hand over his brow like a visor. It helped very little.

The footsteps had ceased. He twisted his neck, peering even harder out the window. He could feel the glass brushing the white of his eye.

He still couldn't see a thing.

The nearest lamp sat on the end table a few feet away. Shutting it off would kill his reflection. Keeping his face against the glass, he reached for the lamp. His forehead squawked across the window, leaving a smudged print on its way. His fingers brushed the dust-caked weft of the lamp shade. The shade fell off the caddy, catching on the wire rim, and tilted away from the bulb. He felt around the base until he found the switch.

And his gaze through the window was met by a dozen or more beady pairs of eyes.

Bellowing a scream that hurt his throat, he shuffled backwards on stringy legs. His flailing arms bumped the end table, knocking the lamp over. It crashed on the floor.

Through the darkness outside, he watched as rows of white stretched across crescent-shaped jaws. They were smiling. Narrow, toddler-like mouths gaped, drooling and savoring.

From the rear of the house, glass shattered. Vincent whipped around, gawking down the hallway toward the crash.

The bedroom. They're coming through my own goddamn bedroom!

He didn't wait for the group outside the living room to break the window. He bolted for the den with all his might. The rug slid out from under him, folding over itself. He nearly lost his footing, but managed to stay up and running.

As he charged into the den, the living room window exploded behind him. *Thump* after *thump* of little feet hitting the hardwood floor followed. And mixed with those sounds he could hear the faint, miniature chatters of the intruders talking amongst themselves.

It's the damn Haunchies from the carnival! They're coming for me! What happened to Leanne?

He saw what he'd originally come in here for standing in the corner. His gun cabinet. It was a two-door, upright locker made of wood and glass. He always kept it locked. Not wasting time searching for the key, he shattered the glass with his elbow. He could feel the burning cuts and scrapes from the shards.

Reaching inside, he snatched his .30-30 lever-action rifle, a trusty weapon since his teenage years, and the *only* one he always kept loaded. He jacked a bullet into the chamber and thumbed off the safety.

He turned toward the doorway as three of the small figures entered the room. They were dressed in carnival attire, bright and colorful. Two were even painted like clowns.

In the light of the room, he was able to distinguish their features much more clearly. The heads cresting their pebble-shaped shoulders weren't much larger than a tomato, and the lower portions of their faces were curved like a banana. Rotting, jagged teeth gleamed from between thin lips on their distorted faces. Their arms were like twigs under their flamboyant clothing, with wicker-thin torsos separating their hollow necks from legs no more muscular than weeds.

Bushels of disheveled and crudely dyed hair jutted from the tops of their heads like the ends of paintbrushes.

He'd never seen creatures so hideous. Almost human, but not quite.

They do look like elves!

Even through their mussed hair, he thought he might have detected minute, pointy knobs jutting through the fuzzy locks. *Ears?* "What did you do with my daughter?" he demanded.

The reply came in the form of ear-piercing laughter. The one dressed in hand-sewn rags stepped forward.

"She's with *us* now." His voice was of a high octave and probably made dogs howl. "Just as you will be, soon enough." He lunged for Vincent.

Vincent dodged the attack and thrust the stock of the rifle in an upward arc. The tiny thing's skull caved under the wooden blow.

A red-haired clown was the next to charge. Vincent twisted to his left and fired. The high-powered slug ripped through red spandex, lifting the creature off his feet. As he spiraled through the air, the bullet exploded from his back.

The exiting bullet slammed into a green-haired clown's throat, ripping open a gulley where his Adam's apple had been. He dropped to his knees, grasping his throat, while blood gushed through the cracks of his fingers. Then he collapsed onto the floor, twitching a few times before becoming still.

Three down.

Vincent hurried out of the den and into the hallway. He cocked the rifle, but the hallway was deserted. He flogged his head this way and that, looking into each room on his way to the stairs. The downstairs appeared deserted. He wondered if they'd fled after hearing the gunfire.

He climbed the steps quickly. His back was arched and stiff, his neck fixed, and his eyes focused forward. The barrel of the rifle was pointed ahead of him as if leading him to the second floor.

At the top of the stairs, he didn't bother checking the guest bedrooms and rushed straight to Leanne's room at the end of the hall. He kept the gun clasped close to his chest.

Ignoring the knob, he used the heel of his boot to kick the door open. The frame splintered as the door shot open. He went inside, aiming the gun.

He froze only a few steps in.

Waiting for him were twenty or more Haunchies piled together, a huddle of crescent-shaped heads twisting to observe him. Standing no more than two feet tall, they were armed with a variety of weapons that looked like they had been constructed by their own hands: homemade pitchforks, machete-like knives, and hatchets made from jagged metal shards twined to wooden handles.

He scanned the room, studying the figures occupying it. Like the three downstairs, these were dressed like carnies. He saw more clowns, other carnie laborers, some even dressed in indistinguishable fluorescent attire, and the sparse numbers of what he guessed were females wore costumes like little dolls.

If Vincent didn't know any better, he'd have believed they *were* dolls that had been crudely crafted.

Raising his gun to fire, he knew he couldn't get them all. But he was going to make sure he got as many as possible.

"Daddy. Stop."

Leanne's voice?

He faced the throng gathered on the bed. They parted like weeds in the wind, unveiling his daughter, lying on her side atop the mattress. Her left leg tapered from under her denim cutoffs and crossed over the right. She was gliding a finger up her thigh. She wore a cutoff, sleeveless shirt that left her midriff bare and, with no bra underneath, he could see the curve of her breasts. He quickly looked away.

She hadn't been dressed this way when she'd left the house. Vincent had no idea his daughter had blossomed so much. To him, she was still his little girl, not the mature woman on the bed.

"Leanne," he said, his voice tired and beaten. "Wha…What is this?" His grip on the rifle loosened.

"They chose *us,* Daddy. They want to stay here. With us."

"What are you talking about?" Another group strolled in behind him from the hallway, trapping him inside. He was massively outnumbered.

"They've been traveling all their lives. They've grown tired of living on the road."

"What does that have to do with us? What does that have to do with *you*? Why are you dressed like that?" Vincent had many questions, but only had enough breath to ask some of them.

"I've been with them, Daddy. All week. When you've been sleeping, I've snuck out to where their camp was on Mystic Lane. Since you were kind enough to let them use our land for their carnival…"

My land.

"…I thought I would go out there and help them set up. Since that day I met them in town, I haven't been able to think about anything else. They've touched me. They love me. They *worship* me."

"What? *I* love you, sweetie. I do. Not them…"

"Daddy, stop. They need me to help take care of them. And I need them too…"

"Honey… What have you done?" He dared another look at her overly exposed body and curves. Dabbled on her skin, along her tawny legs and around her neck and chest, were bruises and scrapes.

Had she allowed the bastards to do this to her? Or had they taken her with force?

Vincent felt his grip on the rifle tightening. He wanted to blow holes in as many of the little bastards as he could. They'd overpower him eventually, but not without a fight. He could probably take down several with his bare hands if he needed to.

"Daddy…I know this is a lot to understand all at once. But this is how it's going to be, whether you like it or not." She sighed as if she were the parent lecturing a child about rules and regulations. "Now, I'm sorry they broke some windows. They were just scared you'd retaliate…and you did, didn't you? So they had every right to break their way in. It wasn't like you were just going to open the door for them."

Damn right about that.

Vincent swallowed the lump in his throat. "I just can't stand by and let them do this to you."

"I thought you might say that." Leanne sat up, swinging her legs around to the front. Her bare feet slapped the wooden floor. "I'm not asking for your permission, Daddy. I'm telling you how it's going to be from here on."

His legs weakened under him. His arms felt like limp and feeble noodles, and he couldn't support the rifle any longer. The gun dropped to the floor as he sank to his knees, his head drooping low by Leanne's bare feet.

"That's better," she said, standing up. "It's so much better if you submit." She kneeled, snuggled a finger under his stubby chin and lifted his head. Looking him in the eye, she said, "It'll be okay. You'll see. It'll all work itself out."

"What's happened to you?"

She smirked. "Nothing I didn't allow." Her tone went stern. "You'll get to keep the house. We'll build our own colony in the fields. The crops will continue to grow as normal, and we'll even plant some of our own. Do you understand?"

He didn't understand any of this, but still nodded anyhow.

"Good. Just keep this in mind: You're only alive because you're my daddy. They wanted to skin you alive and prepare you as our first feast on our new land. It *is* a special occasion."

"Wha...?" He couldn't finish. His throat tightened. He felt sick inside.

"It's okay, Daddy. They're not going to *eat* you or anything. Not anymore." She lowered her hand from his chin, and shook her head as if she pitied him for his stupidity. "I didn't expect you to understand. They've been around the world and have been cultured in delicacies we've never even dreamed of. It's amazing. Their knowledge of the world is *amazing.* They're savages...but are trying to adapt to *our* ways of living. To not feast upon mankind and, instead, focus their appetites on the wildlife like we do."

She stood up, leaving her father gawking at her from his bruised knees. She turned to her new followers, holding her arms out wide as if she were the Almighty Christ resurrected, and, maybe to these brutes, she was. "He won't give us any trouble. He'll supply us with what we need to begin our colony. And we'll do what must be done to survive. No matter what."

"Baby…" Vincent finally said. He collapsed in a ruin of tears.

"Oh…Daddy. It's okay. I love you."

As he sobbed uncontrollably, she returned her attention to the Haunchies. "Bit by bit, we'll reveal ourselves to Doverton. They'll grow to accept us as one of their own, just like my daddy has. They might not like it, not at first, but just like my daddy, they'll learn to coexist."

The crowd agreed with high-pitched howls and hollers.

Vincent could even hear their chatter coming from under the floor. It sounded as if they were everywhere, in the house and outside.

Hundreds of them…all over…

Story Notes:

I debated including this story for a long time. It had been out there, for free, for so long that I didn't think it needed to be in this collection. But I eventually decided it would be okay if this story was a part of it. Plus, it was the first time I wrote about the Haunchies—those miniscule, humanoid monsters that dwell in the cornfields of Wisconsin.

Originally, the story was going to be the opening to *The Lurkers,* which I was calling *Haunchies* at the time. But even as I finished it, I felt it didn't quite belong as the opening. I toyed with the idea of putting it in the middle of the book, as a flashback, and in some older drafts, I did just that. In the end, I decided to go with my gut and remove it from the book.

I was a bit depressed because I had this fun story and nothing to do with it. I pitched the idea to Don D'Auria of putting it up on Samhain Publishing's website as a free read for a limited time. He liked the idea, but thought it might be neat to release it as a free story to coincide with the novel. Give the story its own cover and all. We agreed on it and it was a huge success. My only gripe about it is that Samhain didn't mention anywhere in the description that it was a prelude to *The Lurkers,* or even connected to it in anyway. Sure, at the end of the story was a preview of *The Lurkers*, but that didn't come until after the About the Author section. I pointed this out to Don, and he contacted the marketing department. They told him they'd correct it.

They didn't.

When I was at the Samhain booth at HorrorHound for the first time, I brought it up to the staff. I pointed out how most people stop reading a book when they reach the About the Author section. Since it wasn't a paperback, they had no idea anything else of value was beyond that page and something needed to be added to the descriptions on the websites it could be downloaded from. They told me to send an email to the marketing department and CC them in on it. I did and the error was corrected. But the correction only lasted for about a month, then it was changed back to giving no reference of *The Lurkers* at all.

There were hundreds of reviews for the short story. Some good, but mostly terrible. The biggest complaint that I saw was that the story seemed as if it was setting up something that never happened. It *was* setting up something, or so I'd hoped. And that was the reader's interest in *The Lurkers.*

The positive reviews talked about how much they enjoyed the Haunchies and wanted more stories with them.

Again, these readers probably had no idea there was more Haunchy activity because it was never insinuated that anything existed beyond *The Night Everything Changed.*

I brought it up again to the marketing department, sent links to the several reviews that were proof of my claims, but the efforts went ignored after that.

It was frustrating.

The Lurkers and *The Lurking Season* are the follow-ups to this story, if anyone wants to read more about the Haunchies.

ABOUT THE AUTHOR

Kristopher Rufty lives in North Carolina with his three children and pets. He's written over twenty novels, including *Old Scratch, Pillowface Rules, All Will Die, The Devoured and the Dead, Desolation, The Vampire of Plainfield, The Lurkers,* and more. When he's not spending time with his family or writing, he's obsessing over gardening and growing food.

His short story *Darla's Problem* was included in the Splatterpunk Publications anthology *Fighting Back,* which won the Splatterpunk award for best anthology. *The Devoured and the Dead* was nominated for a Splatterpunk award.

He can be found on Facebook, Instagram, and Twitter.

For more about Kristopher Rufty, please visit: www.kristopherrufty.com

For signed copies of books and more, please visit: www.kruftybooks.com

Made in the USA
Columbia, SC
31 October 2024

45093219R00126